# speculation

## NISI SHAWL

Tu Books

*an imprint of Lee & Low Books Inc.*

New York

TU BOOKS
an imprint of LEE & LOW BOOKS Inc.
95 Madison Avenue, New York, NY 10016
leeandlow.com

Manufactured in the United States of America

SUSTAINABLE FORESTRY INITIATIVE · Certified Sourcing · www.forests.org · SFI-00854

Edited by Cheryl Klein
Book design by Neil Swaab
Typesetting by ElfElm Publishing
Book production by The Kids at Our House
The text is set in Plantin MT Pro

3 5 7 9 10 8 6 4 2
First Edition

Library of Congress Cataloging-in-Publication Data
Names: Shawl, Nisi, author.
Title: Speculation / Nisi Shawl.
Description: First edition. | New York : Tu Books, an imprint of Lee & Low Books
   Inc., [2022] | Audience: Ages 11-13. | Audience: Grades 7-9. | Summary: In 1962,
   ten-year-old Winna Cole discovers a pair of magical spectacles that reveal both the
   friendly ghosts of her African American ancestors and a dangerous family curse.
Identifiers: LCCN 2022022424 | ISBN 9781620149591 (hardcover)
   | ISBN 9781620149607 (ebk)
Subjects: CYAC: Magic—Fiction. | Eyeglasses—Fiction. | Ghosts—Fiction.
   | Blessing and cursing—Fiction. | Fantasy—Fiction. | LCGFT: Fantasy fiction.
   | Novels.
Classification: LCC PZ7.1.S4945 Sp 2022 | DDC [Fic]—dc23
LC record available at https://lccn.loc.gov/2022022424

For Aunt Ruth and
all the Andersons

# Chapter One

It was raining lilacs. At least that's what it looked like to Winna, sitting on her grandparents' screened-in porch. The tiny squares of dark mesh blurred things together, going in and out of focus so silver drops of rain became the flowers they fell on, fell from, and fell all around. Winna took off her glasses to make it more like that, more mixed-up and mysterious. Magic.

Magic was real. Grown-ups and high school kids said there was no such thing, but Winna knew they were wrong. They just said that because they had given up. "You can't give up," she muttered to herself. Mom said so all the time. Even when she had to go to the hospital. Going to the hospital was not giving up.

Winna stroked the spine of the book Mom had

given her. Well, Mom had given her the money to buy it, digging into her purse and trusting her with a whole month's allowance before she got into a taxicab to the hospital and shut the door. And blew a kiss out of the open window as the cab pulled off down the street. Winna hadn't seen her since—two whole weeks.

She left her glasses off and picked the book up from the patchwork quilt she had tucked around her legs so she could sit alone on the cool, flower-smelling porch. She had to put the page way up close to her face, which was supposed to be bad for you. But maybe some of the story would rub off on her. It was called *The Time Garden*. It was by Winna's favorite author right now, Edward Eager. He wrote about magic happening to regular, ordinary kids, just like her. Or almost just like her—they were white.

They always managed to find an enchanted some-thing: a well, or a book, or a coin. Winna was tall for her age (ten), and she was constantly being told to stand up straight and act like she was proud of her height by everyone but Mom, who must have heard the same thing all her life. Winna tried to have good posture, like everyone wanted, but it was hard when she was always looking on the ground for a magic object. A ring, maybe, or a scroll of papyrus inscribed with strange, runic symbols. Meanwhile, there was the book.

The adventures started when Ann, Roger, Eliza, and Jack discovered an enchanted plant that let them travel in time. The magic had just whisked them away to a tropical island, and now they were trying to keep their own parents (who as children had apparently had similar adventures) from being consumed by cannibals for lunch. It was kind of funny, but scary, too, because it made Winna think how if someone eats your mother as a little girl, you don't have a real good chance of being born.

Forty pages passed, and the dangers of cannibals were replaced by those of fire-breathing dragons. Winna tried for the third time to brush away the spiderweb or mosquito or whatever it was that kept tickling her knee where the quilt had slipped off. She touched something soft and squiggly and damp. "Gaahh!" she cried, jumping up on the back of the armchair. But it was only her little sister, Tupelo, who stuck her wet fingers back in her mouth and started crying like the baby she was, sitting on the floor. She was always sneaking up on people.

Winna sighed and rolled her eyes back so she was looking at the dirty white rafters of the porch ceiling. "Can't a person get any *privacy*?"

Tupelo sniffled and took her fingers out so she could wipe her nose with the back of her pudgy brown hand. "But there wasn't nuffin on TV—"

3

"*Anything*. There wasn't *anything* on TV."

"—there wasn't anything on TV," Tupelo amended, "except *Highway Patrol*. And I was lonely." Her dark eyes stared up accusingly.

Winna made an effort to put herself in her sister's place. Not down on the floor, but the way her guidance counselor Miss Ross was always trying to get her to do. Of course Tupelo was lonely, way out here in the country. Well, in Vandalia, but Vandalia practically *was* the country. A church, a barber's, and a post office, which was of course closed for the Memorial Day weekend. No kids they knew for miles around, unless you counted their cousin Benny, who was a year older and a little mean. So Winna would have to play with Tupelo herself.

"Well, what do you want to do?"

"I dunno." But she looked a little better, grateful to be asked.

"You still got that coloring book Uncle Marv gave you?"

"Yeah, but I don't feel like coloring."

After a few more guesses, Winna decided that all her sister really wanted was someone to cuddle with. "All right," she said, motioning with one arm. "Come on up here, big girl. Let me see if I can do anything with that head." She had her comb in her back pocket and she had to twist around to get it out. So she didn't see what happened next. She heard it.

CRUNCH! It was an awful sound, and Winna knew exactly what it meant. Last time that sound had come from under the paws of an overly friendly German shepherd. Now it issued forth from beneath her sister's butt. Tupelo rose right back up from the chair cushion, as if going into reverse fast enough could undo the damage. But it was hopeless. The whole weekend was ruined. Winna's glasses were broken, and that was that.

"Heavens to Betsy."

Gramma didn't seem at all upset. Not compared to the way Mom was, last time. "Those glasses cost me sixty-five dollars," she had said then. "Just how do you expect me to pay for more?" And she had walked out the door, down the steps, and up the block to the IGA, bought some cigarettes, and started smoking again like she'd never stopped. Money was a big deal to Mom.

But Gramma seemed to take what had happened a little easier. Maybe because of all the cookies and pies and donuts she always made. Winna had heard it said over and over: "You are what you eat." If so, Gramma was made of butter, sugar, flour, and eggs. All that soft, sweet stuff kept her from getting mad at the pieces of blue plastic lying there on the dining room table.

They had already tried taping the frame back together, but the results were wobbly. When Winna put them on, the world looked all weird: parts too far, parts too close and leaning over like the sky was going to fall in on her head. It made her dizzy, so they took off the tape and set the pieces back on the table, where their reflections shone quietly in the dark, polished wood.

"Heavens to Betsy," Gramma said again. "Well, pretty soon your grandfather will be back from Paw Paw. He ought to have some notion what we can do."

Winna nodded, but secretly she doubted that. Today was Saturday. Her eye doctor wouldn't be open till Tuesday. Even if he let her come in for an emergency, that was at home, in Kalamazoo, which must be miles and miles away. So she was going to be bumbling around half-blind all weekend. She would miss the fireworks.

But when Grampa Carl came in he seemed to know exactly what to do. He left the box of groceries on the dining room table, overriding Gramma's concern for the finish. "It'll only sit there for a minute, Dot. I'll be back in two shakes of a lamb's tail." He walked into their bedroom, and soon there were funny creaking noises coming from over their heads. Shuffling, slidey sounds, too. There must be an attic, Winna thought.

She walked over to the bedroom and saw that what she had always assumed was a closet door had wooden steps going up behind it, steep as a ladder. A dry, dusty smell drifted down from the top. The wood glowed golden and reddish brown by the light of a single bulb. The string Grampa Carl must have pulled to turn it on still danced in the air. She was about to join him when there was a loud thump and more quick, creaky noises. For some reason Winna decided to go back to the dining room table and pretend she had been sitting there all along.

Grampa Carl didn't suspect a thing. He was smiling under his grey mustache and running his fingers through his curly hair as he walked toward them. He carried a small blue leather eyeglass case and set it on the table in front of Winna.

"These belonged to your Great-Aunt Estelle," he said. "Maybe they'll do the trick, at least till we can get you another pair."

They had silver frames around perfect circles of glass. Two tiny stars pierced the bridge, right where it would rest on Winna's nose. "Those are a pair of real, old-fashioned spectacles, there," Gramma observed.

"Go ahead," said Grampa Carl. "Try em."

Winna lifted the glasses from their case and saw that the earpieces curled almost all the way around, like the kind in pictures of Benjamin Franklin. They were beautiful but different. Reluctantly, she put them on.

It was like stepping into a newborn world. The dim, shadowy dining room became suddenly clear. Dark corners revealed details: clocks, and cupboards, and curious carvings that ran around the walls up near the ceiling.

"Wow," said Winna. She turned and faced Grampa Carl. "Thanks. These are fabulous!" She could see every little curl on his head and how it went, and why it had to go that way. Grampa Carl smiled, and she saw the lines on his face, how they fell into the places they had got used to being in for years.

"Let me see you," said Gramma, on her other side. But when Winna looked at her, she noticed tears. Like dewdrops on a spiderweb, they flickered on Gramma's long, white lashes, then flashed and disappeared. "The spittin image of my sister. Carl, doesn't she favor her?"

"Estelle? I'd say there's a fairly strong resemblance, yes. Question is, as glasses go, do these fill the bill?"

Winna nodded as hard as she could. "They're even better than my old ones. Maybe it was time for a new prescription. Can I . . ." She hesitated, then went ahead and asked. "Maybe if I'm careful you could let me keep them?"

A whimper came from under the table, where Tupelo

was hiding. She always hid under things when she did something wrong, like that was going to keep her from getting punished. But since it didn't look like anyone was going to give her a spanking right away, she had found something else to sulk about.

"I want glasses, too."

While Gramma tried to tell Tupelo how wicked it was to want glasses when the good Lord had given her a perfectly fine pair of eyes, Winna went back out on the porch. The rain had stopped. There were still thin puddles on the dark, wet, wooden steps, but the gravel driveway that curved below them had already soaked its puddles up. Winna walked down the steps and crouched at the bottom. The round pebbles looked pretty, sparkling and polished by the rain. Some she could almost see through, like watery milk. Others had tiny flecks of gold mixed with pink and black.

She'd never noticed before how beautiful a regular old driveway could be. It must be the glasses, she decided. "What if they're magic?" she wondered out loud. "What if these are magic spectacles I'm wearing?"

There was a sort of shimmer in the corner of her eye. It spread so quickly she didn't have time to be afraid. It was all colors, rainbows flying off the edges of everything, as if diamonds had broken apart. As if the whole world was split into a hundred images of itself, each shining brighter than the last. Then the shimmer was gone.

Looking back, Winna realized that this was when the adventure began: not with putting on Great-Aunt Estelle's glasses, or her old ones getting broken, or coming to stay with Grampa Carl and Gramma. Not earlier, and not later. Not that night, when fireworks spangled open and turned flips and somersaults and spun in circles of radiance like stars dancing for joy. It started that afternoon, in that very moment, when she squatted examining the cool, smooth stones, asking herself what made such ordinary things so great. Wondering out loud if magic had come at last into her life. That was when she was caught up in Speculation.

# Chapter Two

The next day was Sunday. Memorial Day wasn't till Wednesday, according to the calendar, but Grampa Carl said the whole week was special. At eleven o'clock in the morning the day was already nice and hot. Ice cubes rattled pleasantly inside the big jar of lemonade Gramma handed in through the truck window. It was heavy and slippery and cold. Winna set it on the seat between her and Tupelo and moved closer to the door. The warm leather cushion was still slowly springing up from where Gramma had sat on the ride to church.

"You want the sandwiches up there, too?" Gramma asked Grampa Carl. She peered into the truck cab, took off her hat, smoothed its white velvet roses, and put it back on her head. "Or do you think they'll be all right in the back?"

"'Course they'll be all right, Dot. No one's gonna bother em where we're going. Enjoy the sermon." Grampa Carl had convinced Gramma that since the entire Sunday school was working on a play about Pharoah's daughter finding Moses in a stream, the girls would feel left out. So he was taking them on a long drive. The sandwiches and lemonade were for their picnic, and Gramma would have dinner with Aunt Pic, Benny's mom. They'd all meet back at the church for evening services.

Grampa Carl started backing out of the parking lot. Winna leaned against the door, checking to make sure it was all the way closed. Gramma saw her and waved, so Winna waved back. "Say a prayer for my mom," she shouted as they drove away. Then she felt dumb. Why had she said that? All Mom had was bronchitis, which was like a bad cold or something, and not really worth praying about.

They drove off the blacktop and the lemonade jar fell over against Winna's leg. She sat it back up straight, her fingers leaving long dark marks on the cool, sweaty glass. "DRINK ME," she wrote, tracing the words in the tiny silver drops collecting on its side. "Condensation," she murmured to herself.

She snuck a look at Grampa Carl. He was sneaking a look at her.

"How's the specs?" he asked. "Any problems? They givin you a headache?"

"No." Winna had decided not to mention the shimmery thing that had happened in the driveway. It was only for a moment.

"How come you ain't wearin em, then?"

"I dunno." She couldn't explain about the special feeling Great-Aunt Estelle's spectacles gave her. She had been saving it for just the right moment in the day. At least, that's what she told herself.

"You got em with you? Put em on. I want you to see somethin."

Winna took the blue leather case out of her beach bag. She had packed the bag earlier on the chance Gramma could be persuaded that almost June was late enough in the calendar to go swimming. She opened the case and looked at the spectacles glittering in the changing light.

"Where you takin us, Grampa Carl?" Tupelo never asked a question if she could whine it. Winna was trying to break her of the habit.

"I thought we'd head on up to Covey Hill."

"What's that?" Grampa Carl didn't answer right away, so Tupelo repeated her question a couple of more times. "What's that? What's Covey Hill? What's that?"

"Layovers to catch meddlers," Grampa Carl replied, and he wouldn't say anything else for the rest of the

13

ride. When she was done crying about that, Tupelo tried to grab Great-Aunt Estelle's spectacles. Winna quickly put them on to keep them from getting wrecked.

They went on dirt roads the whole way. Most of the land around Vandalia was flat and green: green fields full of sprouting corn, green wild meadows, and woods where shadows waited to grow when the green had gotten all the sun it could take in a day. But as they drove beneath one of the stands of cool, protecting trees, the road began to rise. Then it started curving, too, so that if it hadn't been going up so much, it would have been a circle that went nowhere at all. But it went up, and in, and on, past turnoffs to smaller roads, and up and in again.

Finally they came to two old pillars made of stones, standing right next to the road. Grampa Carl stopped the truck with the engine still running and got out. He knocked on one pillar as if it was someone's door, waited a minute, then came back in the truck. Winna wanted to ask what he was doing, but not after how he had ignored Tupelo. He drove past the pillars in silence. The road got worse, all muddy, and the truck rocked slowly up and down as they drove in and out of big puddles in their way. Winna couldn't see why Grampa Carl kept going, and then she couldn't see why he had stopped.

"All right, bootnoses, here we are. Got your specs on, Winna? Good."

Now that they had stopped moving it was obvious what Covey Hill was. It was, or had been, a cemetery. The teetering crosses and headstones seemed sad, as though nobody had looked at them in years and years. Some of them had vines growing over them, which was pretty. The vines were like the veils that hang down from ladies' hats and hide their faces. Lonely faces, hidden from the world.

Grampa Carl got out of the truck, taking Tupelo out on his side. But Winna sat by herself for a minute, listening to the crinkling noises that came from under the hood. The engine was cooling off. She saw curls of heat rise in the air, wavering like ghosts.

"What if there *are* ghosts I could see?" she said, asking aloud. "What if there really are ghosts, and these glasses are so good they make me see them?" There was a sudden rippling before her eyes. When it was gone, she thought at first nothing had changed. Then she noticed a lady in white walking up the hill with Tupelo and Grampa Carl. She was very tall, and her long white dress was blowing in the wind.

Only there was no wind. Winna got out of the truck to be sure. Grass and alfalfa tickled the backs of her knees, springing up from where she had stepped. But the air was absolutely still. It was a ghost. The lady was a ghost.

This was not the sort of magic Winna had expected: dead people, scary stuff like that. The Wouldbegood kids in the E. Nesbit books never had to deal with any ghosts. What should she do?

"Grampa Carl! Grampa Carl!" Grampa Carl turned around and waved. His arm went right through the lady, who stopped. Now Winna could see how she sort of wobbled and floated around. Winna started to cry, which was a silly thing to do. The ghost wasn't hurting anybody. Was she?

"Come on, bootnose," said Grampa Carl. "There's some Coles up this way. Your mama's people are all over here." They sure are, she thought. Even though she was frightened, Winna had to laugh. Over to one side she saw more white shapes moving, blurry because of the tears. She made up her mind not to be afraid. Like some baby. Like Tupelo. She took off the glasses to wipe her eyes.

The ghosts were gone. She polished the lenses as quickly as she could and put them on again. A girl in white was walking away from a group of other ghosts. She was smiling. She was headed straight for Winna.

It was the spectacles, obviously. It was happening just the way Winna had wondered if it might; there *were* ghosts, and the spectacles made her able to see them.

If she didn't want to, all she had to do was keep the glasses off.

But did that mean they wouldn't be there? Or that they *would* be there, only invisible?

The girl in white was really close. She stopped and said something Winna couldn't hear. Her lips were moving, but no sound was coming out. Well, thought Winna, I didn't ask what it would be like to *listen* to ghosts. One thing she knew from reading: magic had rules. She'd better find them out.

"Hi," she said to the girl. "Sorry, but I can't hear a single word you're saying." The girl bit her lip. She made the kind of face you make when you don't want people to know how bad you feel. She shrugged and started walking off, back the way she came.

"Wait!" Winna shouted.

Grampa Carl thought she meant him. "I ain't goin nowhere. Come on, sugar, get that bootnose up here where it belongs."

"Just a minute." Winna was already walking after the girl. The girl was sort of drifting, but Winna had to thrash her way through thistles and raspberries before she caught up with her. She tried to whisper as loud as she could. "Wait. Hey, you. Wait up."

At last the ghost seemed to hear. She stood still, except for wavering a little. Her old-fashioned white dress kept on blowing in the same nonexistent wind as the lady's did, and the lilac-colored ribbons tied at the top of her long black braids moved a little, too, like they would be rustling if they made a noise.

As Winna came closer, the girl turned around and looked back. She had a nice face, wide and round, with dark eyes like deep water and curly lashes. It was funny looking into her eyes, which were calm and steady, while the rest of her kept moving around as if she wasn't exactly there. But the eyes were. Waiting. Waiting for what Winna would say.

"You can't give up. You shouldn't just quit that way," Winna found herself explaining to the ghost. "I mean, we'll figure out how to talk, okay? If it's really important. Like semaphores." Semaphores were flag signals they used on ships before the invention of radio. Winna knew all about them from a report she did in History. "Or we'll use something else, a secret code or something. All right?" The ghost nodded slowly.

"Winna! What's got into you? We can't be waitin here all day!"

"Sorry, Grampa Carl!" she shouted. "Come on," she whispered to the ghost, holding out her hand. It looked like the ghost took it, but all Winna felt was a current of warmth, like when you're swimming in a shady lake and you come to a part where the sun shines.

# Chapter Three

The ghost led the way through Covey Hill. Winna could see how where they went was probably once a path—the tall grass was thinner here, and there weren't any prickers or itchyweed.

The place where Tupelo and Grampa Carl stood was next to a thick patch of plants with long, swordlike leaves. Poking up between were thin stems that held flower buds, fat and dark. The lady shimmered behind them, a worried look on her face.

"Mom loves these flowers," Winna said to Grampa Carl when she got close enough. She tried to pretend she didn't see the lady, since nobody else did. Except the other ghost, who went over and started talking with her silently.

Grampa Carl stooped down and pulled up some grass. "She does, does she? You know what kinda flowers these are, Winna?"

"Uh-huh, irises. They're her favorites. I wish they were open and I could pick some to bring her—"Winna stopped. The glasses were magic, and she knew it was a bad idea to go around making casual wishes in the presence of magic. But nothing happened as far as she could tell—no flowers opened before her very eyes, like in a science film. She decided she'd figure out the rules of the magic as soon as she got a chance to be alone.

"See if you can get rid of some a these weeds, girls. The family used to come up here and clear things away every Memorial Day, but hasn't too much got done lately. Gardenin is hard on an old man like me."

Tupelo sat down and started plucking at the grass blades with one hand. The other hand was in her mouth—the fingers, anyway. Winna knew it did no good to just pick at stuff; you had to get the whole plant, root and all. She sighed, then went behind her sister, digging clumps of twisty yellow roots from the soft, cool soil. The girl ghost came back over and watched.

"Your great-great-grandmother Winona Cole is buried here, girls," said Grampa Carl. "She loved irises, too."

And now she *is* irises, thought Winna. And a floaty

thing that only I can see. She glanced nervously at Tupelo, but it didn't look like she was any closer to bursting into tears than usual. "How do you know this is Great-Great-Great-Grandmother Winona's grave?" she asked. "I don't see any—um—tombstone."

"Just two greats. I guess it *is* kinda overgrown. Up here." Grampa Carl pushed aside a mass of grey-green leaves, and Winna saw the arch of granite showing through. She moved closer to examine it:

### WINONA GONDER COLE
B. 1845    D. 1901
THERE IS NO SORROW IN HEAVEN

Winna did some quick arithmetic. Winona Gonder Cole had died when she was fifty-six. That seemed pretty old, but of course people got much older. Grampa Carl was almost seventy-five. Mom said they were going to have a big party for him at the family reunion late in June. And she would be completely well by then and take Winna and Tupelo.

"Did you know Great-Great-Grandmother Winona, Grampa Carl?" she asked.

"I wasn't much more'n a child when she passed," he replied, "but all the colored around here knew each other at that time."

"What was she like?"

"Well, I don't believe I can say, for a fact. Most of what I remember about Winona likely comes from stories I heard about her. How she got sadder and sadder her whole long life."

"Story! Story!" shouted Tupelo. "I want a story." Grampa Carl looked all around, not like he noticed anything at all. He just looked around at nothing, and Tupelo got the idea. "Please?" she added. "Pretty please?"

"Okay, bootnose. But first let's get back to the truck. Those sandwiches are waitin on us, and I suspect there's some fish need catchin, down at Lawson Lake. I'll tell you about Winona on the way."

They headed down the hill, the girl ghost walking with Winna. The lady ghost waved one wavery white arm. The girl ghost waved back at her. When they reached the truck, the ghost got in the back. What if she blows away, Winna wondered. She went around and climbed in over the tailgate. "Grampa Carl, is this all right?"

"Sure, sugar."

Tupelo stuck her head out the door and squinted at her. "But, Winna, you'll miss the *story*."

"No, she won't," said Grampa Carl. He showed them how the rear cab window slid open, so Winna could listen in.

Everybody got settled. Winna put her arm around the ghost, just to make sure she wouldn't get whisked off. They went slow at first, anyway. Grampa Carl had to back out a long ways to find a turnaround. A couple of times Winna was almost sure he saw the ghost girl. He was looking right at her. But if he had seen her he would have said something. Instead, all he did was tell the story, which went like this:

## WINONA'S TALE

*You two know about slavery, don't you? That's right, people claimin they owned other people, like they would own an animal. In this country it was the whites ownin the coloreds, mostly, and it went on for hundreds of years. Sometimes they'd treat their slaves like a horse, or a mule, workin their bodies down to the bones. Sometimes they'd treat their slaves like pets, give em pretty names and fancy clothes and keep em around to wait table and make the air pleasant with their songs.*

*Winona was born a slave, and taken from her mama when she was just a tiny little girl so she could be one a these pets. That's how she grew up, with bows in her hair and good food on her plate. All she had to do was play with this white child and keep it enter-tained. But she didn't know where her mama was.*

*Didn't even know her mama's name. She swore on the plantation's Bible she would never let that happen to any child of hers.*

*Winona was what nowadays we call a teenager when two important things started up to happen. That's right, Winna, it was the lead-up to the Civil War. The South fought for slavery, the North against it. Now the plantation where Winona stayed was in Louisiana, deep, deep in the South. She didn't know if the war comin would ever make a difference to her, if it was ever gonna make her free. But she knew for certain the second thing would make a big difference. Because she was fixin to have a baby, and that—*

*How did it happen? In the usual manner, Tupelo, and if your mama ain't told you what that is, I'm sure not about to mess with the subject.*

*But when she knew she had a child comin, Winona ran away. Yes, indeed, she escaped and headed north. Most of the men, the overseers and such, were off trainin to fight, but it was still plenty dangerous, and with Winona expectin it was even worse. They were headed up to Ohio, her and some others that had run off at the same time. Even with a guide and lots of help they had to go slow, on foot. And sometimes, she was so tired and sick. Finally, on a farm near the town a Garland, Tennessee, this family that had been hidin* the runaways said she could stay with them and rest till she had the baby and got better. So she did. Picked her last name for some speaker she admired and got ready the best she could to care for her comin child. The woman who was leadin her to freedom was gonna be back and get her with the next group she brung through.

It was a family of white folks she was stayin with. Good people, though. They were riskin a lot, specially by havin a runaway stay with them for a long time like that. They kept her in their barn, in a secret part of the loft where they stored their hay. They brung her food when they did the milkin. At night they let her come out and walk around, but durin the day she had to stay hid in the secret room.

She stopped there two months. Then the baby was born. She stopped another month after that, waitin for the woman to come back and lead her north, gatherin her strength and watchin her baby grow. It was a little boy. She named him Key, on account of it was him unlocked her chains and set her on the road to freedom. She loved her little boy Key for that, but of course she mainly loved him for hisself.

She woke up around noon one day. Before Key was born, she'd got in the habit of sleepin through till nightfall. Nothin better to do in that little room, and *since it was summer it got awful hot and stuffy in there, so usually she slept. But all that changed when she had that baby. Key was a good baby, too, but a baby's got to eat, and his diaper got to be changed, and if his mama's 'sleep she got to be woke. Winona had learned to rouse up at Key's softest whimper, almost before he knew he was about to cry. The quietest sound. But it was somethin even quieter woke her up this time. It was silence. Key was gone.*

*Winona screamed! She couldn't help herself, though she was supposed to be still, in case the neighbors heard and turned everybody in. They'd had their suspicions, accordin to this family, so she hushed herself up quick as she could. She looked all around the room, tellin herself Key musta crawled off under some hay or somethin, though she knew good'n'well can't no month-old baby crawl.*

*Then she smelled the smoke. Then she noticed how hot the floor was underneath her feet and she realized the barn was burnin!*

*The door was locked on the outside, like always. She tried to bust through anyway, but it was too solid. And it was hot, hotter even than the floor. Fire just outside, burnin to come through and get her. But Great-Great-Grandmother Winona hadn't come all that way to die.*

*She grabbed up her blanket and threw it to soak in the water bucket. Then she wrapped it around her and waited for the fire to do her work for her, openin that door. When the fire burned through, Winona ran out between the flames. Next thing she knew, she was standin there starin at the whole farm goin up in smoke: barn, house, kitchen, chicken coop, everything there was, up in flames. No one else in sight. No sign a Key, no matter how hard she looked, how far from the burnin barn she went lookin.*

*She headed north on her own, aimin for Canada, but she settled here. Married Ezekiel Cole and had eleven other children by him. Lived a good life, kind an generous to every passin traveler, helpin everyone she could. But always askin had they seen her baby anywhere on their way. She never gave up lookin for that Key.*

# Chapter Four

Gramma and Grampa Carl's tub was enormous. It stood on four big feet, like dragon paws: pale greenish-blue on the outside, gleaming white on the inside. It was filled with hot, bubble-frothy water—and Winna. Usually she had to share a bath with her little sister, or at least they had to use each other's water. But since she'd missed her nap, Tupelo had fallen asleep in the truck on the way home. She was completely crabby when they woke her up for supper, and Grampa Carl had sent her straight to bed right after. Winna felt a little guilty for not making her brush her teeth, but it would just have to wait till morning.

She scooted down in the tub till everything was under except her face. Water filled her ears and sealed out the sounds of the rest of the house. She heard her heartbeat loud and clear, though, and the gurgley sound of air escaping, rising up from where it had been trapped and tangled in her hair.

Winna couldn't see her without the spectacles, but she was pretty sure the ghost was somewhere nearby. All day the ghost had stuck close, even sitting next to Winna at church for evening services, looking bored and kicking her high boots soundlessly against the back of the next pew.

So the ghost was good, or anyway, not bad, or she wouldn't have dared to walk on hallowed ground.

While Tupelo dug for worms with Grampa Carl that afternoon, Winna had worked on strategies to get the ghost to speak. Was there only a certain amount she could say every day? Certain topics she could talk about? Winna remembered the kids in *Magic by the Lake*. They got in awful trouble because some of their wishes weren't "wet," and they were working with a watery kind of magic. She'd decided she'd better stick to stuff about sight, but that was as far as she'd gotten in figuring out rules. This was her first chance since.

She rolled over and stuck her face underwater, eyes shut tight. A bubble tickled her nose, leaking up along one cheek. A bubble of air in the water, a bubble of water in the air? No, that would be a droplet, water vapor. Like a cloud, like— She sat up suddenly, sloshing part of her bath on the floor.

Condensation! Cool beads of water silvering the jar of lemonade, steam on the bathroom windows, fogging up her lenses—she was thinking so fast it hardly made sense. She grabbed her washcloth and scrubbed briefly at her arms and legs, leaped onto the already soaking bath mat, and quickly toweled dry. Dry enough, anyway. She had an experiment to perform—she couldn't spend all night grooming herself like some dumb poodle.

Winna wrapped her hair in the towel, turban style. She took the spectacles from the window ledge. Through them she saw a world like a pearl, shimmering with possible colors.

"I wish—" No, that was wrong. She had wished for the irises to open up, and they had stayed shut. What exactly had she said about the ghosts? She hadn't wished, she had wondered. "What if?"—that was how it went.

"What if . . . what if I could *see* what the ghost girl is saying?" Nothing. She tried again, louder. "What if I could see what she says to me?"

All that happened was that the steam seemed to part a little bit, suddenly. She took off the spectacles, discouraged. Maybe she only got one wish a day. Or maybe she'd better clean them off and try again. She reached for a tissue from the shell-covered box and stopped.

Words were etched in the fog covering the lenses. The left eye read, *I'm not the one who's deaf, you know*. The right said, *So you don't have to yell*. It worked!

"Is that you?" she asked, looking where she thought the ghost would be.

The letters filled with mist and new ones appeared. *Yes, it's me*, on the left. On the right, *Yes, it's Estelle*.

If only she could see her at the same time that they talked. Still, it was better than before. "I hope you don't mind me borrowing your glasses."

*Wearing them will let you see.*     *Keep them on and you can help me.*

"Help? Help you with what? How?" The air was clearing, the fog on the lenses starting to fade. "Is this the only time we get to talk, when I take a bath?"

There was a knock at the door. "You 'bout ready for bed, Winna?" It was Gramma. "It's almost nine thirty. You got a long day ahead of you tomorrow; you gonna need your rest."

"Yes, Gramma, I'll be right out."

She looked back down at the lenses. Two words

remained of Estelle's answer: *No* and *breath*. It wasn't fair. It didn't make sense. She put the spectacles on, then had to take them off again for a second to get her nighty over her head.

Estelle waited by the door. Was the ghost going to go to sleep now too? And where? It was crowded enough with Winna and Tupelo sharing the same bed.

Cool air rushed through the open door as they stepped into the hall. Winna shivered and dug her toes into the thick grey carpet. The kitchen door was open, and little rattling and chinking sounds came out. Gramma was setting the table for breakfast tomorrow. She did it every night before she went to bed.

For a moment Winna thought about going into the kitchen. It had pale yellow walls, like butter, real butter. She could watch Gramma put everything in place so the next day would be easier to start and go smoothly. But she was supposed to be in bed.

She turned and headed across the hall to the sewing room, where Tupelo was already curled up in a corner of the hide-a-bed. You wouldn't think, to see her all tucked up like that, that Tupelo was any kind of problem to sleep with.

Estelle was looking closely at the new Singer. "You like to sew?" said Winna. "I hate it. I always get a cramp, right here,"—she put her hand on the back of her neck—"and if I use a machine I just know I'm going to run my finger over.

"Come on and lie down," she added. "There's plenty of room." She didn't even cross her fingers; this was what her guidance counselor Miss Ross would call a social lie, and it didn't count. Besides, there *was* plenty of room—for now.

Estelle just shook her head. Probably ghosts didn't sleep, thought Winna. She was going to have to find out about that, too. Tomorrow.

She got into bed and turned out the lamp. The hall light was on in case either of the girls needed to get up in the night and go the bathroom. By the slanting glow that fell through the doorway, Winna saw the ghost sit herself up on a clothes hamper next to the window. Her black braids hung and wavered against her straight white back. That was the last she saw of Estelle before she took off the specs and slipped them into their case beside the lamp. But she kept on talking to her anyway, a little while. "Thanks for letting me borrow your glasses." She closed her eyes. "I'll take good care of them. Promise."

✦

Winna slept until the dampness woke her. One sleeve of her nighty was soaked. It took her a minute to connect this sogginess with the snuffling noises coming from that side of the bed. And the weight beginning to numb her arm from the elbow down. It was tears, not—what she had expected.

"Tupelo?" The crying sounds continued. "Tupelo, you have to be quiet, sweetie, you'll wake up Gramma and Grampa Carl." Probably not, since they were clear on the other side of the house, but it was all she could think of to get her sister to stop. It didn't work.

Tupelo was really going now, getting louder with every sob. Winna sighed, got her arm back, sat up, and turned on the light. Tupelo was all tangled in the covers and sideways on the bed. Her feet stuck out and dangled over the edge. Her fingers were stuffed in her mouth, both hands. Winna wondered what she'd sound like if she took them out. A tornado siren, she'd bet. Tupelo's eyes were shut tight—she probably couldn't even tell the lamp was on.

"Tupelo, what is it? What's wrong?" Winna was starting to get worried now. This could be serious, an appendix or something. Maybe the grown-ups *ought* to be woken up.

"Mo—Mo—M—Mommy!"

"Mommy's in the hospital. You know that, Tupelo."

"I want my mo—mo-o-o-ommy!" The fingers had come out now, and the wordless wail that followed would put a siren to shame.

What should she do? Water—in movies people always threw water on somebody in a fit like this. She ran into the bathroom and filled up a couple of Dixie cups, then ran back, sloshing a little on the carpet. There was still plenty left when she got back in the sewing room, though. Tupelo was sitting up on the hide-a-bed, and Winna got her right in the face.

For a moment her sister was so shocked she forgot to scream. The sudden stillness lasted long enough that Winna heard four soft thuds coming down the hall. Footsteps. Grampa Carl, or Gramma. Somebody was up. They'd be mad, too.

Tupelo started crying again, but quieter, sort of low and whiny and uncertain-sounding. Before she could work herself back up to full blast, Winna tried one more time.

"Shut up!" she hissed. "Just—just hush a minute and I'll—I'll—" She thought wildly. "I'll let you wear my glasses tomorrow."

Silence.

Gramma stood in the doorway. She had on a pink bathrobe over a long blue nightgown. "What's the meanin of all this noise, girls?" She didn't sound *really* mad. She came closer, but it was still hard to tell anything without glasses. "You two were raisin quite a ruckus a minute ago, and now you don't have nothin to say?"

"It wasn't me—" Winna started to explain.

"She frew water in my face," Tupelo broke in. "And tole me 'Shut up!'"

"Well, she was crying so *loud*."

Gramma sat down on Tupelo's side of the bed, then got up quickly as the moisture started seeping through. "Good thing you warned me to put that old shower curtain under the sheets, Winna. Still, we're gonna need some fresh ones. Can you go get em, honey? You know where the closet is."

"Okay." Definitely not mad. Winna picked up the spectacles and put them on. Estelle stood up from her hamper by the window. Had she been sitting there the whole time? She followed Winna out into the hallway.

Actually, Winna wasn't quite sure where the closet with the towels and sheets and things was. At her house they kept that sort of stuff in the bathroom. But when she reached for the knob to open the bathroom door, she felt Estelle's warmth touch her shoulder, and looked up. The ghost pointed down the hall to the kitchen. "That's right," said Winna. "You used to live here, didn't you?" She let the ghost lead the way.

On the far side of the kitchen from the hall door was what Gramma called the pantry. Besides shelves and shelves and cupboards and cupboards of canned fruit and cookie tins and onion bins and pickling crocks, there was a washer and a dryer. Next to them, a closet. "Thanks," she told the ghost.

Everything was neatly stacked in piles, with the smallest stacks on top. There were labels on the closet's shelves: "Tea Towels," "Face Cloths," "Napkins." "Spare Bed Sheets" were near the bottom. They were tied together in pairs with pieces of ribbon, one fitted and one flat. Winna picked a set and headed back. It was almost too easy. "When I grow up I'm going to live in a house just like this." Estelle, walking in front of her, shook her head no. "Yes I will too. How would you know, anyway?"

They got to the sewing room and Winna had to stop arguing so no one would hear her talking to nobody there. But the ghost just kept shaking her head. She was smiling, too. Winna tried to ignore her. It was hard. It made her mad, this smug, know-it-all ghost standing there shaking her head about the future, when all she knew anything about was the past. They couldn't even have a real fight about it until Winna took another bath.

Winna made the bed, feeling grumpier and grumpier.

It was the middle of the night. She was tired. She wanted her own bed. Better yet, her own room. Gramma had Tupelo sitting on her lap on the sewing machine stool. The baby was telling her some stupid dream.

"—an then the monster *took* me, an he *grab* me, an he was gonna eat me all up, wif big red *hair* all over his face, an I try to call for my mommy but I can't *breave* any, an—an—"

"There, there, sugar, it's all right, Gramma's here."

"An anyway, even if I could it wouldn't do no good cause my mommy, my mommy *died*!" She started crying again.

Winna stood very still. She was suddenly sorry she had made fun of Tupelo, even if it was only to herself. That was the worst, the truly scariest kind of dream to have. Mom dead. And because she was already in the hospital—even only for bronchitis—the idea of her dying felt too close to being real. Although when Winna had bad dreams like that, she was old enough to know better than to wake up the whole house.

It was the whole house, too. Grampa Carl came in the room. His robe was black and red, like a hunting jacket. "My fault, Dot," he said. "I'm sorry."

"Sorry for what?" said Gramma. "What did you do, Carl, take this little girl to some horror show in Paw Paw and not tell me?"

"No, I did nothin of the sort; I took em to Covey Hill, like I said I did. But on the way back I told em that story 'bout Winona."

"Carl . . ." Gramma's face crinkled up tight. The lines and wrinkles around her eyes pulled in, as if they were making sure no tears escaped. Her mouth got small and tight, too, but a second later everything smoothed out, and she said, "My grandmother is at rest now, and I don't think—" She stopped again. "We'll talk on this later.

"Winna, reach me my handkerchief from the pocket of my robe. No, not that one; other side. Thank you, darlin; you're such a help."

Winna got back in bed. She watched Gramma drying Tupelo's face and blowing her snotty nose. "Your mama ain't nowhere near dead," she was saying.

"She ain't?"

Winna winced. Once the weekend was over, she'd have to start concentrating on Tupelo's English. It was going to be impossible to keep her speaking correctly with Grampa Carl and Gramma around as examples.

"Prove it to you," said Grampa Carl. "We'll call her up and you can talk to her. First thing in the mornin. All right?"

"All right."

"Now get some sleep."

Gramma laid Tupelo down on her half of the hide-a-bed. Her half. Maybe if Winna used one of her Magic Markers from Uncle Marv and drew a dotted line down the middle of the sheet, she'd get half the bed to herself. It didn't seem too likely, though.

Gramma let Grampa Carl kiss her on her cheek in the doorway when she left. He took the specs off Winna and folded them up in their case. "These workin out for you?" he asked, his hand on the lamp.

"Yeah." She grinned, embarrassed. "I'm getting so used to them now, I guess I forgot I had them on."

"That's good. Real good."

"Maybe—" Would she be bad if she asked for another story? Grampa Carl had said he made Tupelo have her nightmare because of the one he told them this afternoon. But maybe this one would make a happier impression. Besides, she wanted to know, and it would take the ghost forever to tell her anything. "Sometime could you talk about what Great-Aunt Estelle was like when she wore the specs? When she was little?"

"Now! I wanna hear too!"

Tupelo must be feeling lots better. "Ask nicely," Winna warned her.

"Please? Pretty please with sugar on top?"

"Well—" Grampa Carl took his hand off the lamp

cord without pulling it. "Dot's the one you oughta ask, Estelle bein her older sister. But she don't like to talk about her much. Besides, she wasn't but seven years old when Estelle passed on. . . ." He sat on Winna's side and kept talking.

Was the ghost listening? What would it be like to hear your life told as a story? Would you agree with what people said or hate it?

## ABOUT ESTELLE

*Estelle Cole was born on a March morning in 1891. Only twenty-eight years after Lincoln freed the slaves. I know that seems like a long time ago. But I was alive then, though I can't rightly remember everything about them days myself. Me and Estelle were related, of course—not too close, or I'd of never married her sister, but I played with her much as I did with any girl and I saw her at church doings and in the school-yard and so forth.*

*Estelle means star, you know, and she was always lookin up and askin questions about stars, about the skies and what was to be seen in em—which was a lot more back then, though you probably don't believe me. But it's true. But it wasn't enough for Estelle: she*

41

wanted a proper telescope. Said she'd see it all then: comets, and the moons around Jupiter, and Saturn's rings. I heard she was savin up, plannin to buy the parts to build one.

She was good at puttin stuff together, and particularly glass and mirrors and lenses. Even them spectacles—they come from a mail-order catalogue but she fixed em up special. Better. Not that she needed em—only put em on for formal occasions.

One thing she did nobody else in these parts coulda: she up and made herself a kaleidoscope! Me and all the other kids never got enough a lookin through that thing—finally broke it, and didn't that cause a commotion!

See, without movies or TV shows, kids had to entertain themselves. Went swimmin and fishin in the summertime, slidin in the winter—when we didn't have work to do at home. What kinda work? Churnin butter, skinnin furs and tannin hides, dippin candles, makin sausage—sounds interestin, don't it? Believe me it was work, and we were glad to get away from it when we could.

Girls had the worst of it, I admit. Some of em never even got to go to school, which you might say was a big bonus if you were like your cousin Benny. But generally girls who weren't in school were cleanin, cookin, *mindin their younger brothers and sisters—by mindin I mean what you call babysittin nowadays, Winna. Not obeyin em, no. And no, they didn't get paid for it.*

*Even Estelle, smart as she was, folks was talkin about takin her outta school when Winona died. That was Estelle's grandmother. With Winona gone, people expected Estelle should help her mama, Rachel, look after little Dot and Emmanuel—six and four they'da been. But Rachel and Pardon Cole wouldn't have none a that. Sent her away to a fancy school in North Carolina where she took sick and died.*

*Now I done it. I better not say no more. No—well, seein as your sister's asleep and you promise you won't have bad dreams?*

*It was the consumption. Tuberculosis. A very serious illness of the lungs, and by the time they brought her home to Vandalia, it was too late to save her and she died. Eleven.*

*Lotta children passed on young back in those days. You be glad you were born when you were. Modern times have plenty a good things goin for em: medicine, equal rights. Be glad. You're gonna see some wonderful things in your life.*

*Now get you some rest. Goodnight.*

✦

As soon as Grampa Carl turned out the light, Tupelo crossed the imaginary bed-dividing-line and snuggled up to Winna. She must have only pretended she wasn't awake. Maybe cuddling up would keep her from another nightmare, thought Winna. She slipped her arm beneath her sister's head to cradle her closer. Tupelo really had been scared, even if it was for no reason. The doctors in the hospital would make Mom fine. Besides, with all the crying she'd done, it was a cinch her sister didn't have it in her to wet the bed the way she usually did.

Winna wished she could turn on the light and put on the specs and ask Estelle about dying. If it hurt, and why she wasn't in Heaven yet.

The specs. Estelle didn't wear them the way she wore her dress and ribbons. They weren't part of how the ghost thought she looked—but she'd made them? No, fixed them up somehow special—how? Was that why they were magic?

Tiredness was taking over her brain. She would figure it out in the morning.

"Night-night; sleep tight," Winna whispered into Tupelo's fine hair. "Don't let the chickens bite."

# Chapter Five

"Fabulous bike, man." Winna was trying to be nice to Benny. He was eleven, and he could knock the wind out of her with one quick punch. So she stood in front of his house, looking at his banana-seat mini-wheel with the deep-vee handlebars, searching for cool ways to tell him how cool he was to have such a cool, cool bike. Even though she thought it looked kind of dumb, way out here in the country, with milkweed and cows and a barbwire fence behind it.

Could you pop a wheelie, a really good one, on a gravel road? She didn't know, and she didn't much care. She watched Benny's hands, his shoulders. You couldn't tell anything from his eyes.

"Gonna put some sparklers in the spokes, light em up after dark?"

She risked a glance at Benny's face and saw a glint of respect. "Yeah," he said, "that's just what I was thinkin I oughta do."

As if the idea would ever have occurred to *him*, thought Winna. Maybe in a million years. "Can I ride it?"

WHAM! The boy was just too fast. She was sitting in the road before she knew what hit her. Gravel stung her palms, and her wrists burned from catching her sudden weight. But she could still breathe all right. Not a punch, then; probably just a good hard shove. She looked up to where her cousin stood, his stupid bike stuck between his legs.

He laughed. "What you think, this a *girls'* bike?"

All of a sudden Winna was laughing, too. It was Estelle. The ghost had come up behind Benny and started copying him. Same hunched-up shoulders, same quick, jumpy head motions, same jaw sticking out. Plus she could see something else she'd never noticed before: Benny *vibrated*. He bounced up and down, like Estelle was doing now, only not so much. The ghost was doing everything faster, harder, funnier; it made Benny look more nervous than mean, like the deputy sheriff on *The Andy Griffith Show*.

"Hey, Barney," she giggled. "Barney Fife."

Benny pushed his bike up against her leg. "You gonna be laughin on the other side of your face." He rolled it up over her, pressing her knee down the wrong way, then stopped with her leg between the wheels. "Just keep on callin me that name."

"Okay," said Winna. "Barney. Hi, Barney. Barney, Barney, Barney. Fife, Fife, Fife."

He had the back wheel against her leg now. If he rode over her knee sitting on the bike's seat, that was really going to hurt. "Go on," said Benny. "Say it again."

"Say what again?" she asked, stalling for time.

"What you call me."

"BENNY!" But that was someone else, yelling from the house. Aunt Pic, Benny's mom. "WINNA! Get in the truck, kids. We ready."

Aunt Pic was so thin she fit in between Grampa Carl and Gramma, the way Tupelo had riding over. Now both girls sat in the back of the truck with Benny, the big pans of potato salad, and foil-lined shoeboxes full of peanut butter cookies. And of course, the ghost.

They had a folded-up army blanket for a cushion. Winna was glad; her butt was sore from falling on it, and she didn't think she could take much jouncing around.

As soon as Grampa Carl pulled out of the driveway, Benny started jabbing Winna in the ribs with his elbow.

Tupelo, who had been pouting because Gramma couldn't get through to Mom on the phone, whimpered every time Winna bumped up against her, knocked by Benny's blows. Only Estelle seemed unaffected. She hovered over a box of cookies, sniffing the air with a longing look.

Jab. Jab. Aunt Pic opened the sliding window, and Grampa Carl turned his head from driving to yell back at them. "If you kids don't simmer down back there, the barbecue is gonna have to do without us."

"Oh, but my potato salad—" said Aunt Pic. "I promised—"

"I ain't said nothin against you goin, Picquetta. I'll drop you and Dot off, and me and the kids will go somewhere else. Somewhere educational. The library, maybe."

Benny stopped. "Wait," he said to Winna beneath his breath. "Just wait."

Winna waited. She watched the countryside whiz by. Dirt flew up behind them in a long, brown cloud. Benny settled down with a softball and a stiff, new glove. He kept pounding away at the webbing, slamming the ball in again and again.

"Is there going to be a game today?" He ignored her. "You're pitcher, right?" He nodded. Not too much; you could hardly tell he wasn't just bouncing from some pothole. But Winna continued. "I love softball. In that park across from my house there's a diamond. People play there almost every night, in summer. Can I watch?"

"Sure." Well, of course she could; who was going to stop her? What she really wanted was to play, but she couldn't do that to save her life. Then Winna remembered: nobody here knew that.

"Have you got your team picked already? Maybe I could help."

"Uh-hunh."

Some answer. Grampa Carl pulled into the lot in front of the big fieldstone storm shelter and parked. Benny jumped over the side of the truck and ran off before she could ask him what he meant: uh-hunh he had his team, or uh-hunh she could help. Winna and Tupelo were stuck carrying food to the picnic tables.

They must be early, Winna decided. There was hardly anyone else in the park. "Congregation's runnin on C.P. time again," Grampa Carl complained. He folded out an aluminum chair with peach-colored plastic webbing. "It's one o'clock sharp."

The chair was for Gramma. Her "Arthuritis" wouldn't let her sit on a bench all day. She settled in her seat and said, "Try and be a Christian about it, Carl. They'll all be here, another half hour or so."

"What's c-p spell?" asked Tupelo.

"Don't spell nothin, chicken; it stands for somethin," explained Aunt Pic.

"C.P. is short for colored people, like you and me, bootnose," added Grampa Carl. Winna already knew about being colored, or Negro, which was what Mom and Uncle Marv said. And she knew the history of why Vandalia had hardly any whites living in it—back in olden times it had been a stop on the Underground Railroad, the way out of slavery. But Tupelo was too young to hear about that yet. She was still figuring out who was what.

"And colored is like Winna?" she asked.

"Yup."

"And like you, Gramma, and Aunt Pic?"

"That's right," said Gramma, speaking for both of them.

"And like my—my—" Tupelo's lips trembled. "Like my mom—"

Winna jumped up from the picnic table. "Oh, Tupelo, look!" she shouted. "Swans!"

"Where?"

Winna pointed to a wide pond. "There." Four white swans floated on the water. They seemed so sure of themselves, so certain they would always swim at the center of everything.

Before anyone could stop her, Tupelo ran off over

the grass. "Tupelo, wait, you'll scare them—" Winna raced after her sister, but it was no use. The birds rose up, beautiful even in their surprise. The ugly sound they made didn't seem like it could come from such graceful throats. Sun shone through the cupped wings of one that flew right overhead, dazzling their eyes. So Winna didn't see where they went. She looked down at the ground and blinked. There were white feathers scattered on the grass.

"I want my swans."

Winna refrained from telling Tupelo the swans weren't exactly hers. "They're gone for now, big girl. But look, they left something for us. A present." She stooped down and reached for one of the glowing spears of light, then stopped. "You first."

Tupelo took a small, downy feather that didn't even bend the blades of grass it touched. "And one more for Mommy," she said, without a single sob. "This one's pretty." She picked a long, pointy feather. "Now you."

Winna's was a long one, too. She stuck it in her back braid, like the drawings she'd seen of beautiful Indian girls paddling in canoes. Then she picked up a short feather, broad and round like a butter knife, for Estelle.

"Who gets that one?" asked Tupelo.

"A friend. Someone you don't know."

Estelle was with them, had been the whole time. It

was funny how used to her Winna was now. Only yesterday she'd been so afraid.

More people had pulled up in the parking lot. There were a couple of kids on the swing set. Aunt Pic was pushing and giving underdogs. She shouted for the girls to come take their turns. Tupelo left, but Winna stayed where she was. She wanted to try something.

She waved the swans' gift in the air to get the ghost's attention. "Estelle. Psst. Hey, Estelle." Why did she whisper, she wondered—no one else was near enough to hear.

The ghost was walking on water. She stopped and turned around in the middle of the pond. She looked a little lonely standing there on the smooth, dark surface in her wispy, white dress. Floating like a feather.

"Let's talk. I figured it out how—" Winna took off the spectacles. The world got grayer, less interesting. Why had she ever thought that going around half-blind made things more magic? She breathed on the glasses, coating them with mist. Immediately, words appeared:

*I thought that*        *understand.*
*you would*

Both lenses cleared quickly. The condensation didn't last as long out here as in the bathroom.

"Was that what you were telling me when Gramma interrupted us last night?" She held the lenses to her lips again, blowing steadily.

*No, I was asking*         *for a hand.*

"Oh. Well, what did you want me to do?"

*Help me*         *find Key.*

Winna sank slowly down till she was crouching by the pool. She put the specs back on and saw the ghost coming closer, drifting over the water.

"You really want me to do that? You really think I can?" The girl and her reflection nodded. "But listen, Estelle, it's 1962. That baby boy, he'd have to be over a hundred years old now. He's probably dead. He must have died a long, long time ago."

The ghost started talking again, so Winna had to remove her specs and fog them up. Several times.

*No he's not.*         *I know for true.*

*If Key was dead I*         *be standing next*
*wouldn't*                *to you.*

"Why? How do you know that? Anyway, if he's not dead now, he's gonna be soon. Over a hundred—that's old! What's the difference if I find him or not?"

Winona vowed her first baby
  with every child    would be found;

that she would in her arms
  hold him

before his came round,
  dying day

or no one would breathe easy

nor rest within the burying
    ground.

"But—but that was only her saying that! You want me to help your grandmother? Okay. But you never promised to find Key yourself—did you?"

She swore it on the Bible,

so by her we're bound.
  solemn oath

"Everyone? The whole family?" Mom. Mom had to keep an oath she hadn't even made.

> What she said will
> have to be;
>
> even she cannot
> break free.

Winna shuddered and wiped the spectacles off fast as she could. This was like a family curse! A chill crept up the back of her neck. In stories curses came from wizards, or evil witches. The Coles might as well have put one on themselves. Winona's vow was why Covey Hill had so many ghosts. Including Great-Aunt Estelle.

If Key did die before anyone found him, no chance this story would ever have a happy ending.

"I'll help. What do I do?"

> Use the spectacles
> to learn
>
> what to do and
> where to turn.

"Right. But *how*?"

> That's up to you.
>
> The only rule's the
> Rule of Two.

"What's the 'Rule of Two'?"

Suddenly Winna felt weird. She was supposed to help a ghost lift a curse. And Estelle was talking even less like a little girl than she looked like one. All these rhymes, and saying the same thing over again. All the comfortableness Winna'd had about being around her dead great-aunt vanished like fog on lenses. What could she say? What could she ask? In the sudden silence she heard someone come running up behind her, swishing through the grass. She made sure the specs were clean, then hurried and put them back on.

It was Benny, bounding like a leopard, zigging and zagging through the open field. He stopped just before he would have banged into her, barely panting.

"Joanie Jergens got the chicken pops," he announced. "You're first base."

# Chapter Six

On those rare occasions she'd gotten to play before, Winna always wound up in the outfield. Hardly any kids ever hit the ball that far. If they did, she ran in and grabbed it up from the ground and threw it toward home, underhand.

But here she was a few steps from the first base bag, on damp dirt instead of clean grass. She knew enough—from watching the game way out where she was usually stuck—to understand *why* Benny had put her there. Because she was tall. She had a good reach; she should be able to catch the ball and step on the base and tag the runner out easily.

Sure she should. She knew exactly how. She knew

everything about the game. Everything you could learn by watching.

Batters on the other team lined up behind the chain-link backstop. A short fence ran off one side of it in front of a bench full of people, mostly moms and dads of the kids playing. Aunt Pic was there, and Grampa Carl. And sitting next to him on the end, Estelle. Even the ghost would see how bad at softball Winna was.

Benny looked over his shoulder at her like she was supposed to guess his secret meaning. He twisted around quick and threw. Fast. The pitch whizzed past the bushy-haired boy with the bat and smacked in the catcher's mitt with a loud, dry thwack. "Steee-rike!" called Grampa Carl, standing up from the bench. Another grown-up was the umpire, but he didn't say anything, only kind of shrugged his shirtsleeves a little and nodded. Estelle rose up at the same time as Grampa Carl and came across the infield to Winna. Winna worried about the ghost interrupting the game, then remembered nobody else could see her. Except maybe Grampa Carl. But he was probably looking at Winna, not the ghost right beside her.

Benny struck out the bushy-haired boy in three throws. The next batter was big. A girl. She had on high-top sneakers and a striped tee shirt, but a skirt instead of shorts or jeans. She hit Benny's second pitch.

The ball flew high through the air like a satellite, way out to where Winna would usually be stuck at. It only bounced once, right into the glove of the outfielder. Who threw it at her! At Winna! She had to catch it—and stay on the bag—and tag the runner barreling down the base path—

No! The ball went by her outstretched arm— nowhere near the mitt. Benny was saying swear words and racing toward home as the big girl shoved Winna aside like a locomotive and rounded second, heading for third while Winna sat up from where she'd fallen, dazed, eyesight a blur—her glasses? The spectacles! If she let *this pair* get broken—she had promised Estelle—

She groped at a flash of silver metal in the dirt of the base path and found the specs. They were fine. She put them back on carefully and looked around. Estelle was right there. Winna got up, a little wobbly.

Over by the backstop Benny jumped up and down, still shouting bad words. The big girl was shouting right back at him. She knew more curses, too. Her knees were covered with dust and blood. She must have skinned them. She must have slid into the plate. The umpire and the boy playing catcher were backed up against the chain-link, not saying anything. Aunt Pic left the bench and walked around the fence—to do what? Spank Benny? Benny saw his mom and stopped what he was saying in mid-word. He jerked himself away from home and headed back for the pitcher's mound. Aunt Pic talked quietly to the umpire a moment, then went off the field, pulling the scrape-kneed girl by one arm.

Winna could see from Benny's body's tight, fast movements that he was madder than normal. Not at her, though—with his back to the new batter he stared out to left field, his eyes screwed down and angry-looking. "Second!" he shouted. "Next time go to second; got that, dumb butt?"

Though Winna had missed the throw, it never should have come to her in the first place.

Benny got the kid on deck to pop out to third. The one after him hit a hard line drive—right to the short-stop's glove. Three outs.

Winna was at the bottom of her team's batting order. She plopped down by Grampa Carl on the bench and accepted a paper cup of Hawaiian Punch from Aunt Picquetta. She wished Estelle could have some. And her sister would want a cup too, of course, though Winna didn't see her on the bench. So she had to be with—

Over by the shelter, the peach lawn chair sat empty. "Where's Gramma?" she asked. "And Tupelo?"

"Gone to call your mother," Grampa Carl told her. "The pastor lives across the road and he's lettin Dot use his phone, so they'll be back before you know it."

Before she knew what?

"Too bad you missed the cut-off." Grampa Carl was trying to make her feel better about not catching that throw from the outfield. "You need to learn to *see* the ball into your glove."

It was Joanie Jergens's glove, not Winna's, but all of a sudden that didn't matter. Because she understood what her grandfather was saying. And actually, she understood a whole lot more. In fact, she was so busy understanding things she almost didn't realize they were going back out on the field again after only five up.

Winna wouldn't have to be bad. Not now, not ever again. She was wearing the specs; all she needed to do was *use* them and she could *see* the ball into her glove better than anyone else in recorded history. Winna felt like she was floating like Estelle all the way over to first.

She planted her tennis shoes a foot apart in the soft, black soil and leaned over so no one could see her mouth move. "What if these spectacles made it so I could play softball and win?" she muttered. She blinked and thought maybe she should be more specific. You never knew what sort of trouble magic might make. "What if these spectacles help me see so much better I can catch and throw and run and hit the ball *perfectly*?" That ought to do it.

It did. Winna made all that half-inning's outs.

A light-skinned fat boy wearing a man's hat grounded down the line. The ball blazed at her along a track of echoes—no, that was the wrong word; she could see, not hear them. She lowered her glove to where the bright images ended up and the ball rolled inside it obediently. Winna remembered to step on the base and the boy went off dejected to cling to the backstop.

Benny did the look over his shoulder at her again and nodded once. Obviously he believed now she knew what she was doing.

The next batter fouled two grounders and popped the third pitch straight up. "Mine," Winna called, and hoped that was okay by Benny. Out of the blue sky the softball fell, its—its *forerunners*, she decided—falling ahead of it, looping and twisting like a long white chain as she waltzed underneath, both hands cupped and mitt wide open as a heart in prayer. And caught the ball. Caught it.

Two down. The big girl with the skinned legs stepped in the batter's box. It couldn't have been her turn yet. Nine on a side, and the other team's third out last inning had happened after her home run. The big girl had been the second hitter, then the fourth hitter was their final out. This inning Winna had gotten rid of hitters number five and six. There ought to be four more batters, bottom of the order and then the return of the bushy-haired boy at the top, but here she was again. Big, a teenager even maybe.

The big girl took two pitches. The umpire turned his head to Grampa Carl on both of them. "Ball one!" he said. "Ball two!"

Winna glanced left where Estelle drifted back and forth like a tied balloon. The ghost didn't seem as impressed as Winna had expected. What was she staring at across the street?

Crack! A line drive straight between short and third. An outfielder ran in and scooped the ball up and didn't even slow down for the throw to second. The big girl stopped on first. She put her fists on her hips and took a couple of deep breaths, edging off the bag a few steps as the next batter scuffed his feet in the box. And then a few steps more. Was she stealing—

Benny whipped around and Winna thought it was just to give that look again, but here came the ball! She stuck her glove up to where its forerunners went and WHAP! She *had* it. The big girl came charging back to first like Winna wasn't right there on the base path— was she supposed to act afraid? Jump aside? She did, but not too far. With one long arm Winna swiped her glove against the girl's side, then held the ball up where everyone could see.

"Yer out!" yelled Grampa Carl, without even waiting for the umpire to ask him.

Winna felt wonderful. The spectacles had practically made her a hero. Now to learn how they were going to help her hit and run. She went to join the line behind the backstop. Grampa Carl was waiting there. He held out his hand and when she put hers in it, he led her away from the playfield. "Sorry," he said. "Fun's over, bootnose."

"Why?" Winna glanced ahead at the picnic shelter. The peach lawn chair was gone.

For a moment no answer came. "Dot and Tupelo got hold of your mother."

"In the hospital? Is she all right? Is she—can I talk to her?"

Grampa Carl made a funny, rumbling sound, what in a book would be written as "Harrumph." "Sure you can. Why you think I'm pullin you outta the game?"

They walked through the grass and weeds—white and pink clover, and plants like short cattails with tiny clusters of petals on their ends—till they reached the dusty parking lot. Her feet and Grampa Carl's crunched loud on the gravel. Estelle walked in front of them without a sound.

Aunt Pic sat in the peach lawn chair with Tupelo on her lap. In her excitement over making all three outs,

Winna had missed when she left the bench. Gramma was up in the truck on the passenger seat. "Did you tell her?" she asked Grampa Carl.

"Well. No. Thought it might be best if Rachel did that. Get in, Picquetta."

Rachel meant Winna's mom.

"To ride across the street? Daddy, I can walk that far." Aunt Pic was Mom's sister, so Grampa Carl was her dad.

"Carryin Tupelo?" Tupelo had been crying. Which might not be a big deal. It wasn't usually, and she was stopped now. Aunt Pic got up and went away with Tupelo in her arms.

Winna excused herself as she climbed over Gramma to sit on the truck's seat. She wanted to ask what it was Grampa Carl was waiting for her mom to tell her. Only she was afraid to find out.

Her chest couldn't seem to breathe in any air. Her stomach felt heavy and hard, like there was too much in it, and the bumping truck bounced it around like it would break. But the ride wasn't really far. They got out soon, and the pastor's wife held open her house's door and let them in while Aunt Pic and Tupelo were just reaching the sidewalk.

Estelle's face seemed worried. The grown-ups looked normal, though with them it was always difficult to tell.

Winna sat down carefully on a satiny, gold-colored couch. Estelle patted at Winna's hand on the couch arm and sat across from her on the glass-topped coffee table, without messing up the magazines.

Gramma called the pastor's wife Mrs. Day. Mrs. Day brought the phone in from another room and cleared a space for it. Grampa Carl dialed a number and asked to be put through to Mrs. Williams. Then Winna was holding the receiver. The quiet hissed.

"Go on, child," Mrs. Day urged her. "Long distance."

"Mom?"

"Hello, Winna. You havin a good holiday?"

Well, no, of course not. But better not upset anybody. "Yes."

Mom's voice sounded thin and wheezy. "I appreciate you sayin that, baby. Listen, I gotta stay here a little longer so they can work on me some more. You okay with that?"

No. "Sure."

"That's what I thought."

"How long?" Winna couldn't help asking. She only hoped it didn't sound like whining.

"At least another week. And we can't have you miss that much school, so you're gonna move in with Aunt Pic in Paw Paw and go to North Glade. Just to finish the year. Just a couple weeks."

Winna was going to live with Aunt Pic. And Benny. Awful. But she didn't let that distract her. "What's wrong?"

"That's the part they have to figure out. Don't worry—"

"Your lungs?"

"Yeah."

Estelle looked worse than ever. This must be Great-Great-Grandmother Winona's promise. The curse. It was killing Winna's mom.

And she had wasted wishes on a stupid *game*.

"Winna? Say something."

It could—it couldn't—could it be cancer?

"Sweetheart?"

"Okay." What was okay she didn't have any idea. At least a week at Benny's, doing her best not to get beat up. The boy had no—no *scruples*, nothing holding him back. He'd hit anybody: girls, babies—"Tupelo, too?"

"No, she'll still stay with Grampa Carl and Gramma. And you can come visit with them on weekends."

Weekends. More than one.

Winna told her mom she loved her and they made kissing noises for each other and hung up. She wanted to scream, only her voice box hurt so hard from keeping from crying. "No one would breathe easy" was what Great-Great-Grandmother Winona had decided, and it was the same for everyone in her family. Including Mom.

Now she really had to find Key.

Tupelo and Winna and Estelle got in the back of the truck to go home. Not home; to Grampa Carl's. Aunt Pic went to find Benny at the park. They would get a ride and meet back at the house to take Winna with them to their place after she had repacked her suitcase.

Since they were about to be apart a whole week, Winna kept her promise to let Tupelo borrow the spectacles on the drive back. Without them, she couldn't see Estelle, let alone talk to her. That was all right. She had time now to plan what to say. And what to do.

Winna put both arms around Tupelo and let her lean between her legs. Pretty soon Tupelo was napping. Winna wondered if the spectacles were helping her sister see her dreams.

# Chapter Seven

The boys must be waiting for her. Winna was sure. She shivered and rolled down her sweater sleeves. It was afternoon. It had been hot and sunny that morning when she went to school, same as the first two days she'd gone. Now the sky was low and grey and it smelled like any minute it would rain.

Three boys, all her age, and another who was two years older. They had been ahead of her when she took the path across the vacant lot by the pipe store, cutting kitty-corner through the trash and long weeds. Now they were nowhere in sight.

All day they had been mean to her, calling names. With no teachers around, it would be worse.

Winna looked at Estelle. These boys were solid and

alive. Estelle couldn't hit anybody and get them to feel it. The spectacles? Maybe they'd help somehow, if Winna had time to think of a way to use them. . . .

She slowed down but kept walking. Benny had shown her this route Tuesday, her first time coming home to his mom's from North Glade. Wednesday, yesterday, she had walked this way alone and been fine.

On the vacant lot's far side, the path dropped down into a ditch and ran alongside some old railroad tracks. That was where they would catch her, down where the fight would be invisible from the street. That would be their strategy.

She didn't know any other way to get to Aunt Pic's.

How could magic help? Her brain was empty.

She could give up. Retreat. Sit down on the sidewalk in front of the pipe store till the boys got tired of waiting to beat her up or some grown-up noticed her. Go back to school.

"Nope." Giving the ghost a last look, she tucked the spectacles safe in their blue leather case and put the case in her front dress pocket. At least they'd be protected, like she promised.

Then she glanced around—she should have still had the glasses on for this part, but she spotted a big branch anyway, almost a broken-down tree, only a few steps ahead on the right. It was hard and dry, and she snapped a stick off it easily. The end came away pointed like a spear. It reached as far as her arm, maybe even a little farther. She whirled it in the air like a baton and marched forward. Downward.

There they were. All four of them were white, like most people in this town—it was different than Vandalia. They had short, stiff haircuts the same as astronauts. The big one was Ken, and the names of his friends—cousins, actually—were Sam and Tony and Marcus, Tony's twin. Well, everyone said Tony and Marcus were twins, except they didn't look alike, which was what got Winna in trouble, when she asked if they were fraternals. And they thought—Winna didn't know *what* they thought. That she was making fun of their father? Fraternal twins were very scientifically interesting—they had the same dad and mom, just different genes—but it didn't matter. The twins looked different but both mean. They all did. She whirled her spear in the rain-smelling air.

"Oooh! A stick! I'm scared!" said Ken. He held his hands together in a prayer shape and pretended to jerk away when she wasn't even trying to hit him.

"Sticks and stones may break my bones," Tony said.

"But a *black giraffe* will never hurt me!" Like that was the signal, the three smaller boys ran at Winna to knock her down.

Wham! Her spear slammed sideways against some-one's arm. She tripped. The ground was hard. She pushed and got up on her feet again. Her weapon had vanished in the grass. She pulled her dress straight and patted the blue case in her pocket and then they started hitting and shoving again. Four boys against one girl! So mad she was crying, Winna made her hands fists and her arms were a windmill. She didn't care where she hit them, in the nose or on the mouth or anyplace.

Then there wasn't anything in her way. Anybody. Winna blinked and she could see Marcus and Tony's backs and butts and legs scrambling up the ditch's side. And next to her, barely even out of breath, stood Benny. "Yeah, you better run! Try and beat *my* cousin up!" he yelled.

"Th-thanks." Winna couldn't believe she was stut-tering. How stupid. She looked down at the dirt on her legs. Tiny gravel pieces stuck to her skin. She brushed them off. There was blood underneath.

"You okay." Benny didn't even sound like he was asking her. He began walking away up the path and Winna followed him. She felt wet drops on her head, slow, then fast. By the time they reached Aunt Pic's it was pouring rain. Her sweater and her dress and the blue leather case in her pocket were soaking with it. Even her underpants. She had to change her clothes completely before she could sit down in the kitchen for their after-school snack.

She put the case on the kitchen table next to her plate so the leather could dry out. "What's that." She could tell Benny really wanted to know despite how he said it.

Well, she owed him for her rescue. But before she told anything, she checked. Aunt Pic was in the living room with the TV on, watching her show, *The Edge of Night*. Okay. "It's magic."

"Uh-huh."

"No. I mean, yes it is."

"Ain't *nothin* magic. You crazy. A baby." Benny took a big glug of chocolate milk. "Why I gonna believe you?"

Maybe this wouldn't work as a way to pay him back. "Look." She opened up the case and took out the spectacles.

"Glasses. So?"

"So they make me see stuff. Ghosts."

Benny laughed. "Ain't no ghosts! No magic and no ghosts neither."

What would get through to him? What did he care about? Anything? He liked Dick Tracy and *Highway Patrol*. "They're going to help me solve a mystery."

"Hunh." He set his half a sandwich down carefully. "Mystery. What kinda?"

Hah. She had him now. "A missing person." Winna

picked up half of her sandwich. Velveeta with catsup and mayonnaise; she acted like that was her favorite thing to eat in the world. She finished it. Benny still hadn't said another word. Winna examined one side of her pickle chip, green and wavy. Turned it over.

"Who?"

"Who what?"

"Who missin?"

"Key Gonder." Winna held her chocolate milk up so it hid her satisfied smile. "One of our relatives." Not an ancestor, she had figured out—not if he was still alive like Estelle said. And his last name would be Gonder since Great-Great-Grandmother Winona— Winona Gonder Cole, it said on her headstone—had not been married when he got born.

Benny leaned back in his chair. "Hunh." He looked away into the living room at Aunt Pic. He pulled his lips tight and stood up from the table without touching the rest of his sandwich. "Come on."

He took her in the garage. Aunt Pic used the driveway to park and kept her tool bench in here, and the barbecue grill and things like that when no one was using them. Winna and Benny got a little wet again out-doors, but soon they were sitting on Coke crates in a dry corner where Benny had made sort of like an office behind a dead refrigerator. He had a spool table as his desk, and a file cabinet with two drawers missing. He turned on an old flashlight hanging from the wall by its handle. He got a pencil and a school notebook from the file cabinet and laid them on the table.

"All right," he said. He sounded very serious. "Tell me what you know. Start at the beginnin.'"

Winna suddenly wasn't sure she wanted to share any of this stuff. She set the leather case on Benny's desk, took out the spectacles, and put them on. Estelle sat on top of the refrigerator, swinging her legs. How had the ghost gotten up there? How did she stay? Why didn't she just fall through everything?

Winna took the glasses off and breathed on them as if she was going to polish them clean.

*Go ahead and tell.*   *But nothing about me, Estelle.*

So Winna repeated as much as she remembered of what she had heard from Grampa Carl.

Benny had some problems. "Who set the barn on fire? She shoulda heard em."

"Don't you understand? That's what we've got to find out! Whoever burned the—"

"And why come she didn't wake up when somebody took her baby? If it was you—"

"Probably the same people that set the fire stole Key."

"Okay, that's fine. But the whole thing still don't make no sense. How she spozed to *let* them bad people take her baby without she wakeded up? And then they shut the door and lock her in? And she ain't heard *nothin*? No, unh-unh." Benny closed his notebook and banged his pencil down. "No. Don't make no sense. Somebody lyin." He gave her a disgusted look. "Maybe you."

# Chapter Eight

Winna lay wide-eyed and awake on her half of Aunt Pic's bed. What Benny had said that afternoon bothered Winna so much she couldn't get to sleep.

Aunt Pic's husband had been in the Army and died somewhere far away, three years ago. Winna knew she'd met him but couldn't remember exactly what he looked like, or much of anything except how he used to make believe he pulled off one of his fingers and put it on again. He wasn't buried in America, and even wearing the spectacles, Winna had seen no sign of him. Since she and Benny were too old to share, she didn't mind sleeping in her dead uncle's part of the bed.

But she did mind staying awake in it all night.

The electric alarm clock sat where Winna couldn't see it, on the nightstand next to Aunt Pic, who had started making steady phwooshing noises too soft to call snores almost as soon as she turned off the lamp. Winna was sure without looking that it was at least midnight, maybe later. Which meant that for *hours* she had been trying to fall asleep, and she was *not* a liar. Which she had told Benny.

But he was right. Though she hated to admit it.

Benny wasn't stupid. Just mean. He had filled one whole page of his notebook with a list of everything wrong with what Grampa Carl said. Winna had wanted to make fun of his spelling mistakes and backward ees and esses, but basically he was right. Now she thought about it and thought about it, looking up in the direction of the invisible ceiling. Winna *had* told the truth. Not the whole truth, but everything she knew except about Estelle. Which Benny would never have believed anyway.

Winna had told the truth. Did that mean Grampa Carl was a lie?

No. Estelle had asked her to find Key, too, which must mean the lost baby was real, not made up.

Unless ghosts told stories, the same way people did. . . .

Winna couldn't stand it anymore. Slowly and

quietly, she slid out of bed and walked around to look at the alarm. 12:45. By the dial's faint pink radiance she saw Aunt Pic smile, wrapped in sweet dreams. Winna picked up the case with the spectacles but didn't put them on.

Tiptoeing along the hall, Winna felt her way into the kitchen. There, at last, she dared to turn on a light. The turquoise linoleum of the floor gleamed waxily. Ruffly pea-colored curtains shut out the night above the empty sink. An iced tea glass and a saucer sat on the counter, the only dirty dishes.

She donned the specs. Estelle stood by the water heater in the nearest corner. Good. "Stick around," Winna whispered. "I've got a bone to pick with you." The ghost seemed to hear her loud and clear. So that was all right; no risk of waking Benny or Aunt Pic up. On with her plan.

The kitchen was the farthest from either of their bedrooms, but it was close to spotless. Winna had done this sort of thing with Tupelo before, staying up all night, and had never received any punishment for it. That was because of her work, and the notes she left for Mom to find in the morning: "Greetings from the Unidentified Cleaning Objects," they started out. Grown-ups would let you sneak around all you wanted if it wound up being for stuff they liked. So what would that be this time?

The trouble was, Aunt Pic didn't have anything to do all day other than her housework. Unlike Mom and her job at the phone company.

Winna decided tackling the oven would be the most impressive thing she could try, and would also take the least time. She found the spray under the sink and spread paper bags on the linoleum beneath the open oven door. Estelle backed up and floated a whole foot off the floor when Winna began covering the stove's dark insides with nasty-smelling white foam.

According to the directions on the can, the stinky foam had to sit for an hour and fifteen minutes before she wiped it off. Just to be sure Aunt Pic wouldn't get mad, Winna cleared out the spice cupboard and ran hot, soapy water in the sink.

"I really wish you could help me with this," she told Estelle. Careful not to get their contents wet, she started wiping finger smudges off the sides of spice jars. "But all you can do is listen, and spell things out for answers." The ghost nodded. Her blurry, underwater face seemed sad. "So okay. So who did it?" The ghost shook her head as if she didn't understand. "Was it you? Was it Grampa Carl? Who made up that story that I believed and told to Benny?" Winna leaned her head low over the steaming suds, then took off the specs.

*It's not a fib by*
*Carl or me.*

*Use the specs and*
*you will see.*

Suddenly Winna's head hurt, right behind her eyes. Estelle had called him plain old Carl without the Grampa part, which made sense, since he was not the ghost's grandfather. He had gotten married to her sister. Estelle was not a simple little girl any more than the spectacles were a simple pair of glasses. Winna had to figure out a way to use them and find out the truth or—

—or no one born in Great-Great-Grandmother Winona's family would breathe easy. No one.

She let the water out and went in the living room to sit on the couch. The kitchen light made it so she saw enough to keep from tripping over anything. She pulled the deep green afghan up around her shoulders and decided what to say.

"What if I could see who took Key from the barn?" She frowned into the three-fourths darkness. Was that good enough? She tried again: "What if these glasses showed me who took Key away?"

Winna was glad she had left off the pole lamp. That made it easier to see what looked like a movie the spectacles began showing her. A movie in 3-D.

Inside a tall room a woman lay on piles of golden grass. It was almost as dark there as where Winna sat, though probably not night. No windows, but daylight showed through cracks in the walls. The woman looked exactly like the ghost of Great-Great-Grandmother Winona, only stiller, not blowing around. She had her eyes closed at first. As soon as she opened them, Winna realized she had been awake the whole time. Waiting quietly—for what? In her arms she held a wiggling bunch of blankets, which had to be wrapped around the baby. Key.

The light coming through the walls turned orange. As Winna watched, the woman stood up from her grass piles and carried the blankets with her to a dark door. Winna could barely see its knob. The woman—it had to be Great-Great-Grandmother Winona—grabbed the handle and pushed out. A white woman was standing there with a hat on her head like the lady on margarine packages.

Winna followed the vision of her great-great-grandmother and the bonnet lady through the barn and outside it. The lady's hair and lips were the same color as on the margarine, too.

Nothing was on fire. Nothing burned but the red sun, setting behind a rumpled row of trees on the far side of a field of high corn. Stalks and leaves waved all around them as they crossed it. Great-Great-Grandmother Winona and the lady stopped looking over their shoulders the way they had at first. No one could see them now. Instead Great-Great-Grandmother Winona kept pulling aside part of the blankets, and they both kept petting and stroking the kicking baby inside. Winna wanted to peek over their shoulders and see Key—maybe it would help her recognize him as an old man—but the spectacles didn't let her eyes come that close.

In a short while the sun completely disappeared, but the sky was still clear and blue and without stars by the time the cornfield ended. The row of trees made things dark only as long as they walked under them. Then there was a lawn and a garden with a white house in their middle. The bonnet lady hurried them around to its side to a door and knocked. Winna couldn't hear anything, of course, but the door opened.

They went past the man opening it, who was dressed like a preacher, and through another door right after that to a room with two chairs and a table full of books and crucifixes—crosses with Jesus hanging from them—and candles in golden holders. A window of stained glass reflected back candle flames. The bonnet woman sat down in one of the chairs and pulled Great-Great-Grandmother into the other one beside her. So then Winna was where she'd be if she stood behind them, facing in the same direction.

In front of them walked a white man with red whiskers. He wore a black suit, but he had a stethoscope hanging down below his beard, so that must make him a doctor. He said something and held his arms out. Great-Great-Grandmother gave him her bundled-up baby and the doctor unwrapped him. The baby's tiny arms were waving around like he was mad and arguing about something. He turned his face her way with his mouth wide open as if he was crying and Winna finally got a good look. But this just couldn't be Key.

This baby was white.

# Chapter Nine

Winna was almost back in Aunt Pic's bed—had her hand on the covers, ready to pull them down—when she remembered about the oven. Her brain had been too busy figuring out what the specs had shown her to keep track of anything else. Tireder than she'd ever felt before, Winna returned to the kitchen to finish the job she had started.

Which wasn't too bad. The smell of the oven cleaner had died down a bunch. While Estelle watched, she wetted a sponge and wiped away the foam, brown now with burnt grease.

She sat at the kitchen table to write a note about the UCOs, then got up and pulled a chair out for the ghost to sit in. Probably there was no sensible reason to do that, but it made Estelle smile. After signing her note and leaning it against the salt and pepper shakers where Aunt Pic would see it first thing, she stayed sitting another few minutes, too tired to go to bed one more time. She propped her elbows on the table edge and let her chin sag between her hands.

Great-Great-Grandmother Winona had not told the truth. She was the lie. Winna said out loud what she was thinking: "Great-Great-Grandmother took Key out of the barn herself. If he even was her baby." In what the specs showed he had looked like he was white. And yelling—maybe hurting, maybe mad at getting taken away from his real white parents. And what about the fire? Had it happened or not?

Maybe Estelle knew. Her wavering face seemed so serious. Winna took the specs off and blew on them with her moist breath. But what should she ask? With too many questions to figure out, she just laid her head on the Formica and let her eyes fall shut.

Winna woke up back in Aunt Pic's bed. She barely sort of remembered walking in a dream down the dark hallway, holding on to Aunt Pic's hand—when was that? Winna was alone under the covers now, and outside it was light. This was Friday, a school day—she rolled over and saw the alarm clock only said 7:30. All right, but still time to get up. She put on the spectacles. No sign of Estelle.

Winna got dressed and went in the kitchen. Aunt Pic was smiling while looking worried at the same time. Benny had a box of Cocoa Puffs in front of him. No ghost here, either. Where could she be? Where would a ghost go? Back to Covey Hill?

"Thank you for doing the oven for me, sugar." Aunt Pic put a bowl of cut-up bananas by Winna's Tang.

Winna tried to look confused. "Hunh? I don't know what you mean." It was no use, though. If only she hadn't fallen asleep out here. Why didn't grown-ups understand how to pretend anything? Benny gave her a dirty look. Probably he still thought Winna had been telling a lie on purpose.

On the way to school she wanted to explain what she had found out with the spectacles, but Benny walked too fast. One block from the school fence, he stopped and let her catch up.

"Lissen." Winna wanted to talk herself, but she waited for him first. "You have any more trouble with them peckerwoods today, let me know."

The white boys who had tried to beat her up. Winna felt suddenly cold in the shade of the huge maple tree hanging over them. With all her wondering about who ran off with Key, she had forgotten them. "Do you think they—"

"I don't have to think. I know."

"Maybe I better tell my teacher?"

Benny looked at her in even more disgust than usual. "Yeah. Be a tattletale baby and see if I trouble to save your butt ever again." He was gone.

Ken had the same fifth-grade class as Winna, even though he was two years older, because he had flunked out. Tony had Mrs. Summerlott, too, but the other twin, Marcus, was in with the other fifth-graders, including Sam—and Benny, who had also been kept behind a year. So till lunchtime Winna would worry mainly about Tony and Ken.

First came Arithmetic. Winna was ahead of everyone in this, so she felt kind of bored, but relieved, because all the students had to stay in their seats while the teacher went over their exercise assignments. Once she caught Ken looking at her hard and mean, though.

After that, Mrs. Summerlott had a Health and Science filmstrip for them to watch. A girl turned off the lights. On the white screen at the front of the room, a cartoon hot dog and an ice cream cone fought each other. They wore fat gloves and danced around on spindly legs inside a boxing ring that was also somehow a boy's stomach. It was funny. Winna was still careful to watch out in case Ken or Tony tried to sneak up in the dark and hit her or spit on her or something. The teacher had separated those two on opposite sides of the room, so she had to switch her eyes back and forth a lot.

When Winna noticed that Tony's desk was empty, she stood up as fast as she could and walked to the farthest window. She thought she would need to make an excuse for wanting to raise the shade, but right then the filmstrip ended. Nervousness made Winna pull the shade's cord so hard it tore off in her hand. The shade went up anyway. There stood the ghost outside, pressed against the glass. "Yah!" yelped Winna.

Of course no one else could see Estelle. Mrs. Summerlott made Winna sit down again and wrote some words in her attendance book, shaking her head.

The final thing before lunchtime was Library. Winna had already consumed every last interesting book in her school's library back in Kalamazoo. North Glade's was smaller, but different. Older. The ghost had come inside now, and walked along the shelves with Winna. Had *she* ever borrowed any of these books? No, this school probably hadn't even been built yet when Estelle was a little girl. So long ago—

Winna stumbled and fell against the top of a

bookcase. She hit her elbow and it hurt! Muffled laughs made her turn her head and there they sat, Ken and Tony, smiling nastily together. "Watch where you're going, you black—"

"Shhh!" Miss Tooma, the librarian, pointed a finger at them. The boys shut up, but they stuck their feet out from under their table, right in her path. Winna would trip over them if she walked away. Which was probably why she had hurt herself before—because they made her. Her arm seemed frozen in pain, but she wouldn't give them the satisfaction of one single tear. Acting like nothing was the matter, Winna sat down at their same table.

Both boys stared at her with their mouths dropped wide open. Tony was first to get his voice back. "You— you can't—what do you think—"

Ken took longer to talk but made more sense. Sort of. He stood up. "I ain't sittin here next to no Black Sambo tarbaby. I'm white. Pure white." He said it too quiet for anyone else to hear and walked away. Tony tagged after him.

Now Winna truly felt like crying. Not that she expected everybody to fall in love with her. But her arm still hurt, and why were they getting away with calling her names like that? Shouldn't she tell? Wasn't fairness and equal rights more important than whether she tattled to the teacher? And when would she finally get to go home?

Winna looked up from her lap. Estelle had settled into Ken's empty chair. The ghost wanted her attention; she was making the motions of taking off a pair of glasses and breathing on them. So she had something to tell her. Winna fogged up the spectacles and waited for the ghost's words to appear:

I went to ask my
  grandmother

what she said and
  what she'd done.


Someone took her
  to the preacher's

where the doctor
  helped her son


with a
  medicine
  syrup

that made
  him quiet all
  day long.


That is all she
  never said.

Did it make her
  story wrong?


She didn't want to
  cause a problem

for the friend who
  took her there.

> *That's the reason*
> *she skipped*
> *that part:*

> *she was trying to*
> *make things*
> *fair.*

"Thanks," Winna whispered. "I guess I understand." Good thing Miss Ross had explained about social lies being okay. "So am I still supposed to help her? How?"

> *Yes, of course.*
> *Her Vow's still*
> *strong.*

> *Key has been*
> *missing all*
> *along.*

> *So try another*
> *way to see*

> *what really hap-*
> *pened to her Key.*

She had asked the spectacles to show her who took Key. So they must have. They should have. Was the thief someone she saw in that time? The bonnet lady? The doctor? The preacher? And what about the baby being white? The lunch bell rang while Winna was still thinking about what it all meant.

In Kalamazoo, she lived close to Lincoln Elementary. In Kalamazoo, Winna had time to walk home on her lunch break and eat a sandwich her mom had left there for her with a note saying something funny. A couple of times Winna even warmed up her own can of soup.

Aunt Pic packed her and Benny lunches to bring with them. Winna and several other kids went back to the room with Mrs. Summerlott to take their paper bags out of their desks. She lingered with the ghost in the wide, dark hall to the door outside, peeling back her bread. Salami and lettuce, with mayonnaise and mustard. A pop and an orange and a wax bag of Fritos. Good. She took two big bites of sandwich before pushing the door open.

Examining her lunch had made Winna and Estelle the last ones to the picnic tables. Everyone else was already there in a big, shouting circle. "A fight! A fight!" Winna knew who it would have to be before she shoved her way into the ring. Benny and the four white boys were duking it out, and of course Benny was losing, with blood pouring out of his mouth and nose. And crying? No, laughing! Was he crazy? "Yeah you white! Lily-livers!" Calling them cowards! Ken swung a fist and missed when Benny ducked—but even Sonny Liston couldn't have won against these odds.

Winna wanted to help. She reached past the bushy-haired boy from the softball game and grabbed something—Sam's sweater—and yanked it hard as she could. "Hey!" she yelled. "You leave him alone!" She yanked the sweater again and tore it a little, got a better hold on it, and pulled so hard the white boy fell on his butt on the concrete.

"Hey!" she yelled again. "You quit!" Her voice sounded too loud. Because no one else was making any noise. The shouting had stopped. She looked around.

The other kids were backing away, making room for three grown-ups walking toward her: Mrs. Summerlott and Miss Tooma and the principal.

# Chapter Ten

Aunt Pic came to drive them home. She showed up at the principal's office after what seemed like an hour, but according to the big clock on the wall above the desk was only fifteen minutes. Then she spent a long time in the inner room of the office while Benny and Winna and Estelle sat on green padded chairs too high for them, out with the secretary. Winna heard Aunt Pic's voice through the door and the principal, Mr. Banke, answering it, but she couldn't understand the words they said. That was another fifteen minutes.

Winna had told the grown-ups everything the white boys said and did, but it was like they didn't even bother to listen. Ken and Sam and Tony and Marcus only had to say they were sorry to her, and to Benny when he got back from the nurse cleaning his cut face and stopping his nose from bleeding. Then *they* went back to class, while *Winna and Benny* waited to be sent home. And waited. And waited.

Finally Aunt Pic came out again. She still had on her hat, the one she always wore to church, with its net of diamonds glittering over her dark hair. She smiled at Winna, the same smile as at breakfast, which made Winna feel bad for the first time. "Come on, chickens. Let's go."

Aunt Pic told Benny to lie down on the back seat so his nose wouldn't start bleeding again. Winna rode in front next to the window, with Estelle by her left side. Winna wanted to play the radio—Mom's car didn't have one. But it felt like she might be in too much trouble to try. It was quiet until they pulled in the driveway.

"I made Mr. Banke telephone your mother," Aunt Pic said with her foot on the brake. She shifted to park and shut off the ignition. "The doctors wouldn't let her stay on for long."

Winna couldn't think of what to say. Her mom hated fighting. She said it was exactly what people expected of you, and counter to Dr. King's philosophy. She said when you got in a fight that meant you had sunk to the enemy's level and given up.

"So she'll be calling to talk to you in a little while,"

Aunt Pic continued. "Sometime tonight, after dinner, after I bring you over to Daddy and Mama's."

Aunt Pic made spaghetti and garlic bread and salad with French dressing. Neapolitan ice cream for dessert. Winna looked at her plate and knew it was good, it was food, she should want to eat it. It might as well have been piles of Play-Doh.

The sun was still up when they got to Grampa Carl's and Gramma's, but Tupelo already had on her pajamas. Winna changed into her nighty in the sewing room they were going to share again, with Estelle watching and Tupelo talking about making pickles and planting flower seeds in Gramma's garden. Then they returned to the living room to be right there when the phone rang. Only it didn't.

Tupelo fell asleep on the sofa after two games of Candyland. Gramma left to take her evening tonic and lay out things in the kitchen. Grampa Carl fished the Monopoly board out of the hall closet and bet he could beat Winna. Her heart wasn't in it, and they only went around four or five times.

"I said, 'Your turn,' bootnose."

Winna jumped in her seat as if she had been doing something wrong. Well, she had, but not then. Just looking out the door at the porch light with moths batting around it.

"How you doin with those spectacles?" Grampa Carl had started packing away the money and houses without even asking her if she wanted to quit. "Are they helpful or are they causin you problems?"

Beyond the porch was so dark. Probably by now it was too late to expect her mom to call.

"Still no headaches? Your eyes ain't started smartin? You seein everything all right?"

Everything? Did he *know*? "They're . . . okay," she answered cautiously. She slid the box's lid down and it emitted a soft huff of air. Maybe he *could* tell her *something*. "Grampa Carl . . ."

"What, bootnose?"

"Do colored people ever have white babies?"

Silence. She stole a sideways look at Estelle. She hadn't told the ghost about that part.

"Help me get your sister in bed." Grampa Carl leaned above Tupelo where she lay underneath a cotton quilt.

"But do—" She stopped. Grampa Carl was frowning, making a shushing sign with one finger over his mouth. Keeping quiet, she followed him into the sewing room and turned down the covers on her sister's side of the hide-a-bed.

"There." Grampa Carl tucked Tupelo in. "Now. About that question of yours . . ." He looked around the room, right past where Estelle perched on the clothes hamper. "Guess I'll sit here on the bed. You might as well hop in yourself while we get this straightened out."

Obediently, Winna got under the blankets, but she stayed sitting up, her knees like mountaintops.

"Can coloreds have white babies? In a way, but you have to realize that not everyone who looks white *is* white. Least, that's what the law will say. And colored people, well, we ain't pure Black African ourselves, or not at this point in time anyways." He nodded at Tupelo. "Fine hair like hers come from Europe. That's on account of the way we been forced to mix our blood with whites."

Winna understood. Colored people were all shades, midnight to light tan and everything in between. But Key—if that's who the spectacles had actually shown her . . . "But can someone be colored when they're blond with blue eyes?"

"Sure enough."

Winna let Grampa Carl hand her the case for the specs, but she kept them on as she lay down. "So who decides whether or not people like that are white?" If you couldn't tell by looking . . .

"The laws say one drop is all you need. One drop of colored blood, one known Negro, one bootnose in the family tree—we're some mighty powerful people, if you care to look at things that way." He shook his head like he wondered what the world would come up with next and started to stand. It took him a while.

"Grampa Carl?" Winna was almost afraid to ask what she really wanted to know. He stopped in the doorway. Not almost afraid. But if she didn't find out she'd never fall asleep. "Why didn't my mom call tonight? Is it because she's . . ." Dread swallowed the word she'd meant to say. ". . . because she's too sick?" That was as near as she could get to it.

"Child. No." Tears sparkled in his eyes. "I swear. We wouldn't hide that from you. Couldn't." He took in a big breath and brought his chest up, his shoulders back. "Get a good night's rest. We'll talk to your mama in the mornin." He stepped into the hall. "And be nice to them spectacles. Treat em right."

With a last glance at Estelle, Winna placed her glasses in their leather case and shut it tight. She shut her eyes, too—nothing to see in the hallway's light now without the spectacles. Not that she expected to do anything but lie there awake for hours.

At least Mom was all right. Sick, but alive. The curse hadn't taken her yet.

When Winna opened her eyes again it was daytime. During the night she had turned over to face her sister; Tupelo was already awake, her brown eyes wide, her mouth filled with her fat fingers.

"Hey, big girl," said Winna. The bed was dry. Such a relief. Tupelo smiled around her hand. "Let's get dressed for breakfast."

Since it was Saturday they put on shorts. Tupelo wanted to wear a pink blouse that was too good to play in. Winna let her. She didn't have the strength to argue.

The kitchen smelled like pancakes. Gramma pulled a whole stack of them out of the oven. "Good mornin, girls. You wash your hands yet?" Of course not. Back to the bathroom. But it was worth it for pancakes, warm, with butter, and a decision between strawberry jam and honey. Winna had both. In the middle of thirds, the phone rang.

Winna set her fork down on the tablecloth next to her plate. She heard Grampa Carl answering in the living room. It wasn't polite to eavesdrop, but if that was her mom, Winna *had* to know. "May I be excused?" she asked. Gramma nodded. Tupelo and Estelle got up with her.

She stood watching from the hall, holding onto the other girls' hands. Grampa Carl sat on the couch, the black phone balanced on his pants knee, nodding. "Uh-huh. That's right. Yep. Yep. Right." He looked up at them from beneath his thick, grey eyebrows. "Hold on a second now, Rachel. I believe there's someone here wants to speak with you."

So it *was* Mom on the other end.

"That's fine. Fine. Let me put her on for you."

She sat down next to him and accepted the receiver. "Hi. Mom?"

"Winna?" The voice on the phone was soft and weak, almost a whisper. "What's this I hear about you beating up some white boys?"

"No, Mom, it wasn't like that—"

"You know better. We aren't—" A big breath, before blowing out candles. "—hoodlums. Living in a slum."

"No, Mom. But I can ex—"

"Winna. Be a good girl. I love you."

"I love—I love you, too."

"Give me back to your grandfather."

"All right. Bye. I'll be good." She handed the phone to Grampa Carl and wiped her eyes with the back of one hand. He put an arm around her.

She couldn't cry. It would make Tupelo want to.

Grampa Carl said goodbye and hung up. Tupelo was standing in front of him. "Wait! I didn't get *my* turn!" She tried to snatch the phone away. When Grampa Carl got up Tupelo stretched, but he was too tall for her to reach it. So she jumped on the couch, knocking Winna on the carpet. Winna grabbed her sister's legs to pull her off, too.

"Girls! Girls!" Grampa Carl had the phone out in

the middle of the room, away from all the furniture. "Simmer down! You might wanna talk to the next party I'm fixin to call."

"Me first!" shouted Tupelo. "Me! Who is it?"

"Your daddy. Ought to be late enough in California he'll be awake by now, Winna, don't you think? Winna? Winna?"

She sat up on the couch again. Her head was nodding. "Sure," she said.

If they were calling her dad, things must be even worse than she'd thought.

She let Tupelo go first. During Winna's turn, Dad asked her if they wanted to come stay with him in California after the family reunion in June. To live with him and Ann, his new wife, and all five of her kids. Neither girl had ever been there before or met their father's new family.

Winna didn't want to go, but to be polite she said okay.

After they hung up, Tupelo disappeared from the living room. In another minute Winna heard her whining coming from the pantry past the kitchen and across the hall, above the sound of the washing machine. Hopefully she would spend the rest of the morning helping Gramma. Or at least not being too much of a bother to her.

Winna sat on the couch with Estelle, thinking about the mystery of Key and how fast she could solve it. In time for the reunion picnic? It helped to know that a colored baby could look white. What should she ask next? And who? Estelle hadn't helped with that part. But Grampa Carl had. He knew lots from living to be so old.

The front screen door's spring twanged as it opened and in he came. He sat down at the living room table and took a paper and some mail from under his arm and settled down to read. She stood up and the ghost did, too. They went over to look at the front page of the *Chicago Tribune* Grampa Carl had open. The headline said "130 Dead on Paris Runway" in big scary letters.

Dead. Like Mom would be if Winna didn't find Key. Why had Great-Great-Grandmother Winona made her own family pay for someone stealing her baby?

"Can I ask you another question?"

Grampa Carl lowered the paper. "Somethin more about whites and coloreds? Go on, shoot."

"Not exactly that, but I was wondering. . . . Do people ever make promises that turn out the wrong way for them? Like a vow they can't keep and that has bad . . ." What was that word Miss Ross used? ". . . bad consequences?"

He shook his head. "All the time, bootnose. It's a

sad fact a life that people don't always take care an do right by themselves. There are times they do plain wrong, get in their own way, hexin and cursin their own selves. Like Rachel smokin her cigarettes in the face of the American Cancer Society warnin. Like Winona wishin—well, I ain't gonna get into detail there.

"People like that need help. But sometimes I despair." He picked up the paper again. He was reading the middle section. "Look at this mess in Albany. Won't them prejudice people ever do right?"

"In New York?" Albany was New York's state capital.

"No, in Georgia." That was right; Mom and Uncle Marv had just been talking about a place down South with that same name. "White folks need to get over themselves. Coloreds ain't gonna stay satisfied forever with makin peaceful protests."

Winna came to sit at the table, too. "But Dr. King says violence backfires and gets you in worse trouble than you were before."

"Hmmm. That's true. To a certain extent. Eye for an eye; it's a vicious cycle, bootnose." He folded up the paper and laid it down. "King's got some good points. On the other hand . . ."

Minutes passed. "Grampa Carl?"

"Sorry, bootnose. I was just rememberin a fight I got in with some white boys, a lot like you an Benny's. . . . "

So Grampa Carl had hit back like Winna did? Like Mom said not to? "What happened?"

## CARL'S STORY

*You understand how coloreds are what's called a minority in this country, don't you? Most of the US is white folks, the way Paw Paw is, but growin up in Vandalia, I had the feeling bootnoses was the rule and whites the exception. Even at the age of twelve, when I knew better in my head, my heart kept on tellin me we was the main attraction.*

*Course Paw Paw was the bigger town, even back then, and they had things there we didn't. Drugstore, dry goods shop—that'd be like a five-and-dime nowadays—train station and telegraph, courthouse— all sorts of reasons coloreds had to bring their business into Paw Paw.*

*Felicity—my little sister, she's passed now—she convinced me to walk eight miles with her to Paw Paw because they was sellin a new brand of soda at the drugstore and she had seven pennies saved up to buy two bottles. That's what I said: eight miles. Half as far as to Kalamazoo. No other way to get there so we walked. It was summer, hot, August; don't get no hotter. And dusty—we was coated in grit by the time* we got to the drugstore's back door and asked them to—no, we couldn't go in there—this was Jim Crow times and there was laws to stop colored people doin the same as whites. Still are, lotsa places.

You through askin questions? Gonna let me tell this my way?

Turned out this new soda cost four cents insteada just the usual three. Felicity couldn't buy me a bottle for myself like she'd promised, so we shared. Way before we reached home walkin them hot, dusty roads, that bottle was empty, soda drunk up and nothin but an icy memory.

Then we was crossin over the bridge and I got my bright idea: goin swimmin in the river. Felicity was all for it. We found a path down to the bank, followed it till we knew couldn't no one on the road see us. We didn't have swimsuits. Didn't need none—we was brother and sister, and our underwear was good enough.

But for some folks our underwear wasn't good enough, nor us neither. While we was playin in that cold, dark water these three white boys come up and yelled at us to get out! Only white folks was allowed to swim there, they said.

Now I hadn't seen any sign about that, and I said so. "You tellin me you'd be able to read what it said if there was one?" asked a fella in a wide-brimmed hat.

*Then they were all callin us names and orderin us out at the top of their lungs and threatenin to bring the sheriff down if we didn't quit pollutin their water. Like we colored kids hadn't ever swum in that river before, and upstream from there to boot.*

*I charged outta the water mad as fire! Three-to-one is bad odds, but Felicity was right behind me, nothin but nine years old and a girl, too—she showed em! Shoved the youngest so he landed on his sittin-down-place right in the mud. I had only hit the hat-wearin fella twice and the other one I had tripped, skinny boy with freckles on his face who was gettin up to come at me again, when Felicity pushed my wad a clothes in my hands. "Run!" she said, and she was right. We coulda licked them boys, licked em good, but it wouldn't a done us anythin but harm. Beatin up whites. No, we got away and we was lucky. They musta not told no one, shamed cause we was littler and one a girl. Otherwise we coulda been killed in the night, our families, too. Murder? Yes, there was laws against that, Winna, same as now, but the law woulda somehow seen nothin.*

*Lucky. Yup. We sure was. Whole towns been burned up for less. Can't tell you why ours wasn't.*

*Things is changin. What I hear from Picquetta is at least you and Benny received an apology.*

# Chapter Eleven

Tupelo had kept the swan feathers they found on Memorial Day. She showed Winna where she had hidden them, inside a sewing pattern for raincoats on the bottom shelf of the bookcase in the room they slept in. Pretty good, for such a little kid.

Winna laid the white feathers out along the ledge of the screened-in porch window. Nearly noon, now, and the shade of the horse chestnuts barely reached over the roof. No wind; the feathers' soft fuzz stayed utterly still. Estelle sat in the armchair alone. Only a ghost could stand so much stuffing around her in this heat. Winna and Tupelo shared the metal lounger Grampa Carl had brought in from the shed, shifting from place to place as the green-painted surface warmed beneath their skin, seeking the fleeting coolth.

Four feathers. Winna's was long, and sharp at the end. Like the one Tupelo had picked to take to Mom. Maybe they could mail it. Mom had sounded so much sicker on the phone. When Winna asked if she could visit her mom today, since there wasn't any school Saturdays, Grampa Carl and Gramma only said wait and see. Which always meant no.

But nobody had said anything more about sending them to California since Daddy's call this morning.

Winna definitely didn't want to go and live with five other strange kids! After Grampa Carl's story she had found a little bit of privacy in the bathroom to think and talk to Estelle, and now she knew what to do next.

But when would she have a chance? Being good like she had promised Mom meant more than keeping out of fights. It meant taking care of her baby sister when Gramma was too busy.

Tupelo turned the page of Uncle Marv's coloring book, revealing two new pictures. The first showed an alligator with long curly eyelashes wearing a hat, a purse hanging from one stumpy arm. In the second, a shark in a suit jacket and glasses smoked a cigar. "You can do that one," Tupelo told Winna, pointing at the shark. Maybe Benny would have liked it. Winna took green and purple and orange crayons from the jar on the floor and made the suit plaid. She colored in the lenses of the shark's glasses. Now he looked cool, a gangster or a beatnik. She added a patch of black beard under his grinning teeth. Way better than what Tupelo had done. The alligator's hat was a pink like calamine lotion, and crayon marks crept outside all the lines.

Maybe Winna shouldn't have done such a good job. But before her sister could feel jealous, Gramma appeared with lunch on a tray for them: tuna and macaroni salad, carrot sticks, and Kool-Aid. When they were done, orange Popsicles for dessert. Then Gramma said for Tupelo to take a nap—but not Winna. Finally she and the ghost got to be by themselves again!

"Okay," she told Estelle. "Great-Great-Grandmother told everyone about the fire and stealing Key, and not about when she went to the doctor, which was what your spectacles showed when I asked who took him. But what I actually need to see is the stealing, so now that's what I'm going to ask to watch."

She had thought hard about what to say, and exactly which words to use. Which was how she had figured out the Rule of Two. Repetition. Every magic thing Winna had gotten out of the spectacles, she'd wondered about twice. So that was it. She was sure.

"What if these spectacles showed me what happened

the day Key disappeared?" And a second time, almost identical to the first: "What if these spectacles showed me what happened the day Key vanished from the barn?"

Shadows spread from the trees outside. A soft wind followed the dimness in; the feathers fidgeted restlessly on the ledge, then lay still, their glow slowly fading.

As Winna's eyes adjusted to the gloom, she saw Great-Great-Grandmother Winona back lying on the piles of golden grass. The blanket bundle containing Key rested in her left arm, still bulging around like the baby was in a fight. With her right hand, Winona reached inside her blouse and took out a glass bottle with a black syrup sloshing around inside. On its label, big red letters spelled "Rx," like a sign at a drugstore.

Great-Great-Grandmother pulled a rag out of its top with her left hand while still holding her baby. She took a big sniff and stuck out her tongue and poured a few drops of the syrup on her tongue's end. Then she stuck her finger in the bottle's opening and turned it upside down a second. The finger came away black and sticky-looking; she put it toward her baby's face—in his mouth, Winna guessed, since it came back clean. She got it sticky with more of the syrupy stuff and gave it to Key again. And again. Each time he got less wiggly. At last he quit moving at all, and she stopped the bottle up with the rag and laid it down next to her on the grass pile and fell asleep.

For a long time nothing else happened. Winna felt like she might fall asleep herself. It was so hot. She lifted her hand to take the spectacles off. But then the door of the room they were showing her opened and someone sneaky tiptoed in.

Winna had a hard time seeing who it was. Light only shone between boards, the way it had before. There was barely enough to tell that this was a man. Then he came nearer to Great-Great-Grandmother. He had a hat on, and a beard covered the bottom of his face. He bent over. The beard was red. The doctor.

The doctor! He straightened up holding the wrapped-up baby and tiptoed out.

Winna was furious. How dare he! Now she knew! She wanted to wake up Great-Great-Grandmother Winona and tell her who stole Key. Of course she couldn't. What she was seeing had happened a hundred years ago. Nothing about it was going to change.

Winna sat back on the lounger. She'd gotten up without realizing it. Walking around was probably dangerous, since all the spectacles let her see right now was the past. Should she take them off?

No. Last time they had stopped showing her stuff on their own.

Had the doctor set the barn on fire? How would Winna find out? She wanted to follow him with her eyes. She tried. Nothing happened.

"Estelle!" Winna needed help. "How can I get these things to—to take me someplace else the same day?" Of course the ghost wasn't going to be able to answer her unless Winna fogged up the spectacles first. She pulled them off to breathe on them and their picture shrank, spinning around, falling— So that was it! She stood up again and held the spectacles so she could see through the lenses without having them on. Outside the barn now and high above it like a flying bird, Winna watched the doctor walking fast through the cornfield.

Below, nothing burned, so it hadn't been him setting the fire. She turned and twisted the spectacles around in front of her like a steering wheel. Where were the people that lived on the farm? In a farther-off field, a white man tied a horse to a tree stump and hit him to make him try to move forward. On the other side of the barn, a house stood with curtains blowing out of its open windows. Winna stooped to her knees and swooped quickly through. Nobody home. A long driveway ended up as a bridge crossing a creek. Bushes grew beside the water. The bonnet lady and another white woman plus a group of kids, different ages, seemed to be picking berries, eating them and collecting them in pails.

Winna turned the spectacles to circle around to the barn again. There! A shadow moved along the back, ran behind a smaller building. She chased it, leaning left and right. Another white man—not the doctor or the horse-hitter—wearing blue overalls and a brown hat and carrying—a lantern? In daytime? Maybe the fire didn't have anything to do with stealing Key at all? Maybe this running and hiding man started it—

"Winna Williams! Have you lost your natural mind?"

Winna blinked her eyes and lowered her hands. She folded the spectacles up and curled her fingers over the lenses. Gramma lowered herself onto the lounger and tugged Winna to sit next to her.

"Sorry, child. Was you playin some game with my sister's spectacles? I know you been feelin lonely, but those ain't no toy, and you need to take better care. . . ." Gramma patted Winna on her shoulder. "But I didn't mean to speak so sharp."

Winna peeked inside her closed fists. She couldn't tell anything except that her palms were getting sweaty. "Please, Gramma . . ." Please what? Please go away so she could find out what else had happened while the fire burnt down the barn?

Gramma patted Winna's shoulder again and sighed.

"Things'll get better soon. You'll see. We're havin Pic bring your Cousin Benny by here to play awhile tomorrow after church."

Great. A whole extra afternoon with Benny.

Although that meant she'd get to talk with him a little earlier about the answers she had found so far to the mystery. She'd get to ask him his ideas on how to find that baby-stealing doctor.

Actually, it really *was* great.

Cousin Benny liked mysteries. He could help her figure out where the doctor took Key. Together they would solve everything. Winna wouldn't have to go to California, because her mom would be completely healthy and coming home from the hospital. The sooner the better.

# Chapter Twelve

Outside was the summer: plump clouds high in the soft air, green lawns full of clover, songs of birds running like silver water out of shadows and into the shining of the sun. Inside was Winna. Not playing. Working.

This was Wednesday. Every day so far this week she had been kept after school for not paying attention in class. Which at least solved the problem of how to avoid the four beaters-up. If she looked out the school library's windows, Winna could see where Aunt Pic had her car parked, waiting to drive Winna home.

No. Aunt Pic wasn't going to take her home. Only to where Winna was staying, at Aunt Pic's house.

The outside doors down the hall crashed open loudly and Winna heard squeaky rubber steps running toward her. Benny burst into the room, out of breath and smelling like mud and grass. She shut the book about pioneers in Tennessee she was trying to read, the same one she'd had in front of her all three afternoons. According to Grampa Carl's story, Winona had lost Key in Tennessee, but Tennessee was a big state. The book probably didn't belong in a kids' library; it was fat and full of words that were long even for her. Also, though, it had a photograph in it of a house that looked like the preacher's. Maybe the author said his name somewhere and maybe something about the doctor too, if they knew each other, or maybe some other clue. It was a chance.

"You ready to go?" Benny ignored Miss Tooma and talked only to Winna. He didn't like any teachers. Winna was starting to understand why. The ones here always acted as if she were stupid.

But it was still hard for her to be just plain rude to grown-ups. "May I be dismissed?" she asked.

Miss Tooma twisted to look down from her stool. She had been taking old pictures out of a high glass case. On top of it sat Estelle, her head almost up to the library ceiling. Winna hadn't seen how the ghost got there.

Miss Tooma nodded for Winna to leave. "Is your practice over, Benjamin? Keep it up—you'll be another Willie Mays!" She smiled. But Benny was a pitcher. He never played outfield.

In the dark hall Benny pulled her between two pillars. "I thought you was such a smarty-pants. Why come you messin up in school so bad?" He really wanted to know, and it was all his fault.

"I'm doing research, trying to find out where's that missing person."

"Yeah? Look like you need some help. I let you meet me in my office after supper."

Estelle rode in the back seat with Winna and sat on the hot stove while they ate. Aunt Pic could definitely cook. Fish sticks and French fries and corn on the cob. A little puddle of spinach sat on one side of Winna's plate. She kept its watery juice away from her nice, crispy potatoes by sacrificing one for a fence.

After they ate and washed the dishes, Aunt Pic sat on her couch to watch Bob Newhart. Winna and Benny both had homework, but they only did the first parts before heading out to the garage.

Benny turned on his hanging flashlight and a cricket Winna hadn't noticed was chirping stopped. He fished his pencil and notebook out of the cabinet drawer and slid two stacks of Coke crates nearer the spool table.

"Take a load off." Winna shared her seat with the ghost. Benny flipped the notebook open and stared a while at what he'd written in it last time. The cricket started chirping again.

"We pretty sure we established the offender." Benny nodded to himself. "Yeah. But without a positive ID on him it ain't helped you find the victim." Sunday afternoon Winna had explained to him about the doctor. So Benny had made up a way for her to have learned things that didn't involve magic: letters and diaries he pretended she'd found. He was very stubborn.

Though he had some good ideas too. Benny was why she'd started looking for the doctor in that pioneer book.

"Now you gots too much to handle with all that research, doncha? Tacklin both leads yourself ain't leavin you no time for doin nothin else. Legwork take a long time. You need for me to do some."

Winna tried to tell him the truth again. "It's the spectacles."

"Hunh. Right."

"It *is*. I look through them to see what Key was doing—"

"The victim."

"Yes, him. So I watch his life. Where he went. What he—"

"Wait a minute. You tellin me you watchin your victim's *whole life*? From a *baby*?"

Now she was getting somewhere. "Uh-hunh, and that's why I can't spend time on homework—"

"You really that *dumb*?" Benny bent over and started rocking back and forth, shaking like he did when he was angry, and then he laughed out loud. At her! He sounded like a hyena.

"I am not dumb!" First the teachers, and now this boy who didn't even get good grades! Winna's head was hot with her hurt feelings. She stood on her feet. The Coke crates fell over and she kicked them away. Benny could hit hard and fast but if she had to—

But the ghost got in the way, sticking up her hands, shaking her head and looking scared.

What if Aunt Pic told Mom about Winna fighting Benny and that made her mother even more sick?

Okay, no hitting.

Winna picked up her crates and put them back together while her cousin yipped and hooted and pointed at her. She sat down. "Fine. What would you do, then, Mr. Barney Fife?"

He leaned forward and slapped his hands on the tabletop. "I *tole* you not to call me that!"

"Sorry." She knew she should be.

"Think you so smart." He sat up straight. "Answer

me one question: even if you *do* got magic glasses, how long it gonna take you to watch that whole baby's life till he a old man?"

Winna stared at her cousin without answering him. Because there was nothing to say except what an idiot she was.

Benny snorted and got up from his seat. "Didn't think about that, now, didja?" He yanked the file open, stuck his pencil and notebook inside and slammed it shut. He turned off the flashlight and left Winna and Estelle sitting by themselves in the dusty dark.

It had been interesting to see the doctor and some lady he acted married to, playing with Key and giving him baths and dressing him. It proved they were somehow at least kind of nice, that they at least wanted to be a good mom and dad, even though they didn't have any other kids.

But if Winna looked through the spectacles at only half of Key's life, it would take her fifty years. Even if she only looked at one day out of every week of his past, it would take *too long;* he would be dead before she found out where he was now. Key would die before she could fulfill Great-Great-Grandmother Winona's promise, and Mom—

Winna wasn't stupid, she *wasn't*, she—

"Oh." So stunning was the realization of what she

should do she said it out loud, though no one except the ghost was there to hear: "All I have to do is ask the spectacles. They can show me where Key is *right now*!"

Excited, she jumped up to go inside. No—she sat back down. Why not use the spectacles here, this moment? "Oh, Estelle!" Everything was going to be okay.

Winna repeated her wish, just the way she was supposed to. "What if these spectacles could show me Key where he is? What if they made me see Key where he lives right now?"

Brightness like a reflection filled her eyes. Pale green walls replaced the dim, spiderwebby garage. An old, old man sat in a wheelchair by a window. He wore dark brown pants and a long-sleeved shirt the color of Black Cherry Kool-Aid and spectacles almost the same as the ones Winna had on, only of gold metal. No one else was in the room with him. This must be Key.

Where was he? How far away was the green room?

Winna pulled the spectacles off enough so she could turn them to look out Key's window. A city. Which one? In the distance a sign shaped like a giant loaf of bread wrapped in a red-and-white bag spun on top of a tall pole. Yellow letters stood inside a blue oval on one side, and below that there were more. She zoomed in to read them: "Franz," the sign said, beginning the name with a curly-topped capital F. Then it said

"PREMIUM WHITE" to the right, then something littler underneath—

"Hey!"

Winna nearly dropped the specs. "You! You stop—stop sneaking up on people!" Like Tupelo always did.

Cousin Benny frowned. "I ain't sneakin up on nobody. I just walked in my own darn office! What you doin still here? Mama sent me to say time for bed."

Winna folded up the spectacles' frames. "All right."

"Yeah, but you ain't answered my question. What you doin?"

Winna sighed. "You wouldn't believe me if I told you." She got up from her Coke crates.

"How you know?"

Because she had already tried *twice* now. But, okay, Benny did deserve a break for helping her realize a better way to use the spectacles. And maybe the third time would do the trick. She opened them up again. "It's these. They're magic, honest. They *are*. And you were right, it would take too long to watch what Key did every minute of his life."

Benny snorted a laugh. "Yeah."

"So instead I used them to see where he is this very second."

"You located the victim?" His voice sounded

interested and serious. "For real? Where he at?" He switched on the flashlight and opened his file drawer.

"Uh, I'm not—I need to find out more about—I was in the middle of—"

"Oh." Benny shut the drawer again.

"But I have clues!" Winna added desperately.

Benny cocked his head like a spaniel. "Clues? What kinda?" He opened the drawer once more and retrieved his pad and pencil. Winna told him about her vision of the bread sign and he wrote it down.

"Seem like that might be somethin we wanna follow up on. Anythin else? Street signs, restaurant names?"

"Not yet. I was getting ready to search the area . . ." When you interrupted me, she thought, but what she said was something else: "Why don't you take a turn?"

"Me?" Benny put his pencil down. "What for?"

Winna held out the spectacles and he took them. "You're the detective." Would it work? Could she get her cousin to admit magic was real? "You have stupendous powers of observation."

He lifted the spectacles up and moved them this way and that without putting them on. Their glass and metal glinted in the beam of light shining from the wall.

"No, you have to wear them first," said Winna. "And make a wish."

"Hunh." Benny set the spectacles on the bridge of

his nose and hooked the round earpieces in place. He looked suddenly cooler, like a wise doctor or a bird specialist.

"Now you say how you want the magic to work for you. Twice."

"But what if they ain't no magic?" And before Winna could stop him or snatch them off his face, he said it a second time. "What if these spectacles just jive, and ain't one drop of magic even in em?"

And the spectacles were ruined.

# Chapter Thirteen

Somehow Winna made it through the rest of the week. She checked to be sure the spectacles didn't work anymore. They didn't. Cousin Benny had wondered away their magic. When she looked through their lenses the world was plain and ordinary, even worse than she remembered. Like it was coated in dust, like a chalkboard cleaned with dirty erasers. And nothing she said made it any better. She couldn't speculate them back to the way they were. The magic was over.

Winna missed Estelle. Even though she knew the ghost might be sitting right next to her in class, she couldn't see her. Or anything else important. Anything that would help her save her mom.

Friday was the last day of school. Winna didn't care.

On Saturday Aunt Pic drove her back to Grampa Carl's and Gramma's. Not home to Kalamazoo.

Not to the hospital.

Winna asked Aunt Pic if they could go there, but only one time, in the car, after she already knew what the answer would be. Aunt Pic had the windows rolled down and the radio way up, tuned to a Paw Paw station playing Ray Charles. "No, chicken," she shouted, shaking her head. The wind rippled her bright orange headscarf. "Not today. You wait till you get settled in again at Daddy and Mama's before you try takin a trip into town. Besides, the doctors don't want Rachel seein anybody this weekend."

Static drowned out "Georgia" when Aunt Pic swerved around the curve of the fluttery-flowered apple orchard just before Grampa Carl's and Gramma's driveway. "Why not?" asked Winna, but too softly for Aunt Pic to probably hear. Maybe not seeing her mom was punishment for letting Benny wreck the specs' magic.

They pulled up by the front porch. Tupelo sat on the steps, sucking her fingers. She took them out to yell. "Gramma! Grampa Carl, they're here!" Winna hugged her little sister without wiping her hand off first. At least nobody was sending them all the way to California. Yet.

Gramma wanted Aunt Pic to stay for supper, but

she had to get back by the end of Benny's practice. She had given Winna two of her old madras shirts that got shrunk to kid-sized in the wash. Winna followed Grampa Carl as he carried the suitcase in and put it on the hide-a-bed in the sewing room. It felt crowded and empty at the same time. All that stuff. No ghost. He looked at Winna watching him from the doorway. "So, bootnose, them specs still treatin you all right?"

"Noooo!" Winna wailed. Crying hard, she ran into his hug. "No—they—no, I let—" Not enough air to sob and say words at the same time.

"There, bootnose, you're gonna be fine, now, fine and dandy."

Grampa Carl's overalls were new and stiff against her cheeks, turning softer where they got wet with her tears. His flannel shirt arms smelled like the beginning of night. For a while Winna couldn't stop crying. She wasn't sure she wanted to. How long could she act little like this?

But after a few minutes she slowed down some. "Better now?" asked Grampa Carl. He gave her a handkerchief with purple edges. "I'm thinkin we oughta retire to the attic and talk for a bit before sittin down to eat."

What a good idea. Tupelo was helping Gramma in the hot kitchen; Winna heard her sister asking if she could open the oven as she followed Grampa Carl into his bedroom. He took her into the closet with the hidden ladder and clicked down the light cord. The golden wood glowed. Winna climbed up after him.

At the top was a long space like a triangle, the underside of the house's slanted roof. A window in a wall ahead of her let in the setting sun. Grampa Carl was walking toward it, creaking the old floor. There was a path he took between stacks of cardboard boxes and tall baskets and chairs in pairs, one upside down on the other. And lots of other stuff, but Winna went past it, too.

To a rug, a carpet with designs in red and brown and black and cream and a quiet green. No boxes cluttered up this area of the attic; it was like a living room, with two chairs pulled together so people sitting in them could have a discussion. But the shelves beneath the window held a collection of weirdness—the more Winna looked, the crazier the things there seemed: tree branches, and statues of African people, and brown jars with red wax tops. Around a clear bowl of water on the shelves' top, a circle of fat white candles burned. Grampa Carl was lighting the last one of them as Winna joined him.

"Have a seat, sugar. Either one you want." Winna picked the rocker. "Now what you got to tell me?"

It was hard to start, but it got easier as she went, because Grampa Carl believed what she was saying. Because he believed in magic, too. Because he did it—all that weird stuff was what he used. He understood everything. The ghosts, the curse, the mystery—everything.

He leaned over in the other chair and put his elbows on his knees. "Us Hawkes call it 'the Burden of the Coles.' Self-hexin, like I tole you, Winona and them getting their own way. We been tryin to help with it, marryin into the Cole family line again and again. My cousin Rachel—Dot's mama, the one your mama's named for—she was a Hawkes till she married Pardon Cole, who was the fourth son of Winona. And then my sister, Felicity, married Emmanuel Cole—Dot's brother. And I married her. . . . Been doin the best I can with herbs and tonics, keepin her breath comin easy, fendin off sorrows. . . . Took us nineteen, nigh on twenty years to bring forth a livin baby." He shook his head, staring at the floor. "But only a Cole's gonna be able to end this once and for all. Keep Winona's promise. Redeem the curse. And Dot don't hold with conjure—magic, that is."

"Redeem the curse?" Was that what Winna would have to do?

"Means not only get rid of it, but make it come out right. So how Winona cursed herself—and everyone after her—is still part of the story, but changed to become a blessing."

But how? "But since I let Benny break the spectacles . . ." More tears gathered in her eyes, hurting till she let them spill all out.

"Aww, bootnose. Try not to cry no more; it ain't like you knew what was gonna happen, now is it?" Grampa Carl reached out to her face. "Lemme see can I fix those things up for you."

Blurrily, Winna looked up. "You think you can?"

He winked at her. "Who gave em to you in the first place? You ever wondered about that? Estelle made those spectacles of hers special—and I made em magic."

Of course. Grampa Carl had known what was happening all along. If anyone could help, it would be him. For the first time in days and days, Winna smiled.

She gave the specs to Grampa Carl and he set them on a space on the shelves by the circle of burning candles. "Let's leave these here overnight till I can get some direction on what to do."

Winna nodded. "Who's going to tell you?" Did he have a ghost like Estelle with him? Even better, she found out.

# MAKING MAGIC

*Could be any one of a number of spirits tells me how to take care of them specs for you. I don't know all their names; lotsa that kinda thing was lost durin slavery times. Useta be whole families give themself to followin the teachins of one of em or another; like as not that's what triggered the interest of certain spirits in Winona's vows. Maybe why they wound up so keen on Estelle's doins too, she bein the same line.*

*Most of the spirits I deal with are people I was related to, by blood—and none of us knows who they was more'n a few generations back—or by affection, bein close to em durin their lifetime. Or by their accomplishments, what they did. Though there's some that's natural, guardians of certain plants, animals, places, and so forth. First one I saw was like that— slippin offa my Gramma Rutha's back porch as I came up through the woods. Otter spirit. He was huge—long as I was tall, and I tried to make myself believe he was a dog or a baby bear. Nothin of the sort, of course. Gramma Rutha was out there biddin her friend farewell and she seen that I seen him leavin and she took me inside, told me the truth. Started in teachin me. That was when I was only eight. Same year Dot was born.*

*No, I wasn't too young. You ain't, is you? Estelle was your age when she first fixed up them spectacles. And I was not much older myself when I got hold of em. 1903. All this time they been waitin for you to use em.*

*So you want to know how I done it? Like I said, Estelle was the one who worked on em to begin with, though I don't believe she knew what she was doin. Her mama and papa, Rachel and Pardon, had sent away in a catalogue to buy em from this outfit back East. Estelle took em all apart and calculated the best shape for the lenses, ground and polished the glass till it was righter than before. And as she was polishin she prayed. She wanted them specs to show her what she needed to see.*

*No, I ain't about to tell you exactly what that was, Winna. Some matters are always gonna be private. I will say it didn't go the way she expected.*

*I know what I know.*

*I wound up with the specs about a year after Estelle passed. Rachel gave em to Gramma Rutha as a memento when they buried the child. Gramma Rutha gave em to me; she could feel they had a flash to em—a special shine, a spirit light you could call it. She wanted to see what I'd make a that.*

*I had me some fun: seein into the future, into the*

*past; seein into other people's lives. People who had passed on, like Winona vowin her vows. I even seen into some white people's lives—yes, that's right, got me some respect, and some protection for Vandalia, too. I admit it. That's why there weren't no serious repercussions from me and Felicity wallopin those boys by the swimmin hole.*

*What kinda adventures? There's things it's easier to show than tell you, and I'll wanna check in with your mama before I get too specific. Suffice it to say I was usin the power of these spirits I call the Twins, which is why these here specs are bound by the Rule of Two. Twins got a partiality for two-ness—for twin brothers an sisters, sure, but also for other kindsa pairins: hot an cold, never an forever, husband an wife . . .*

*When I knew that because of Dot's thinkin on hoodoo I wasn't gonna be havin no more visions through the specs myself, I set em so they'd be ready for you. Or whoever else wanted to switch the magic back on. Seems it worked. Till now. But don't you worry none. Leave it to me. Everything is gonna wind up how it should.*

Grampa Carl got up from his seat and so did Winna. They went down to the dining room to eat pork chops smothered in gravy, and green beans and beets and turnips and hot buttered biscuits, and Winna had two servings of everything, even the vegetables. Apple crisp for dessert.

Winna understood about brother-and-sister twins. In Kalamazoo there were Christine and Corinne, who she'd met at an art class at the Douglass Center. And of course Tony and Marcus in Paw Paw. But what did Grampa Carl mean when he talked about those other kinds of "pairings" he had said were important to his spirits? Were they just ideas? Like opposites? Like before and after? That part of what he'd said kept her wondering till she fell asleep.

Tupelo peed the bed, but only a little, and Winna didn't mind much, not really. She cleaned it up mostly by herself, and all Gramma had to do was start the dirty sheets soaking in the washtub.

They went to church early the next morning and watched the Sunday school's Moses play, which Winna couldn't see too well. Then there was the whole regular service to sit through before she had a chance to check with Grampa Carl about whether the specs were magic again.

Gramma stood talking with some other ladies on the church steps while Tupelo tugged at her hand. Winna went to the gravelly parking lot with Grampa Carl and he held the truck's door open as she climbed up onto the shiny seat. Before she asked a word, he shook his head. He shut her door, walked slowly around to the other side, and opened his. He got in and gazed out through the windshield.

"You can't—can't fix them?" asked Winna.

"Lookin mighty doubtful. Benny—you say he's the one speculated how they were nothin special?" He turned to Winna and she nodded. "That little boy's more powerful than he thinks—his daddy was a Hawkes, too, and what he undone I can't just up and redo. Like Humpty Dumpty."

Back to feeling awful again. "Poor bootnose." Grampa Carl put his arm around her and slid her closer. "Listen, we might have the Rule of Two on our side."

"Repetition?" Winna asked.

"Repetition. Let's see if I can . . . this'll be somethin a little bit like an echo. Probably the new magic I give em won't last real long . . . but better than nothin. Right?"

"Right." Winna wanted to know more, but Tupelo and Gramma came and got in and they had to shut up about magic. Gramma didn't hold with hoodoo. Grampa Carl kept his arm over Winna's shoulders and drove home using only one hand. He disappeared up into the attic without asking her to come with him.

Gramma wanted the girls to learn to crochet. Both of them, even Tupelo, who it turned out actually did it better than Winna, maybe because it wasn't so boring for a five-and-a-half-year-old. Winna held the hook and the yarn up close to her nose and got a headache looking at it anyway. As soon as she could, she excused herself from the living room to go to the bathroom. She didn't come back.

Instead she slipped into Grampa Carl and Gramma's bedroom. But the door to the ladder wouldn't open. It must be locked.

She lay on her stomach on the nubbly white bed-spread with her shoes hanging off the side and stared at the blank blurriness of the unbudging door. What if what Grampa Carl was doing up there didn't work?

Steps sounded over her head, then from behind the ladder's door. Grampa Carl opened it and winked at her without smiling. He sat on the bed beside where she lay. His hands were empty.

She asked him anyway. "Are they all fixed up?"

Grampa Carl pursed his lips. "Sorta."

Winna's heart squeezed tight. Maybe—

"They will be, after while."

After while. "Not now?"

"Nope." He sighed. "That Benny . . ."

"So when?" Winna knew her voice had become

small and babyish. This was all her fault. Still, she felt disappointed.

"They're gonna be ready by the family reunion, June twenty-third."

Winna remembered her mom talking about that a million years ago. "Your birthday is then."

"Yep. My seventy-fifth. And that helped."

Winna knew what he meant. "Like when you make a wish on the cake candles." She sat up, still with her feet hanging carefully over the side of the bed.

"Exactly. Earth returnin to its spot where I was born in, and good wishes all around. It'll be a good time. But till then we're gonna have to leave them specs to rest on the altar." He went to the bedroom door and twisted its handle and turned around. "Think you can hold out that long, bootnose?"

Winna nodded yes, staring down. It was easier not to look in people's eyes since she was almost half-blind. All through the rest of the day and dinner and evening services, no one could see what Winna was thinking. Which was that it would be hard for her to wait two whole weeks for the specs to work again, but she could do it. It would be possible for her. But probably not for Mom.

Magic was real. Winna had proved it. But maybe magic wouldn't be able to give her what she truly needed the most: her mom, well again. Maybe it would take too long.

When she had to fight those four white boys, magic hadn't helped her then, either, and she'd needed a big stick. And her mean cousin Benny.

She couldn't just give up. She thought and thought. She hardly noticed eating or brushing her teeth or helping Tupelo put on her pajamas.

When she was sure her little sister and everyone else in the house had gone sound to sleep, Winna slipped out of the bed and went to the bathroom. She turned on the moon-shaped lamp over the sink. "What can I do?" she asked Estelle. The ghost *had* to hear her—unless she had given up and returned to Covey Hill. Winna breathed on the medicine cabinet mirror and covered it in silver mist, but of course no words appeared there. It was only ordinary.

For now, everything she had was ordinary. So ordinary things were what she would use.

# Chapter Fourteen

Whump! Cousin Benny shut the big, thick book of maps so loud everyone else in the library jumped in their seats. "It ain't in here," he announced. He glared at the book like he hated it, like he blamed it for everything wrong in his whole life.

Winna had finished with the last phone book on the second shelf. She sat back, lowered its black cover carefully, and stood. "Okay, let's go then," she whispered across the table. She could come search through the final shelf of phone books later on her own, and check again by herself for stuff on doctors in Tennessee. Better leave before some grown-up kicked them out. Even the squeakiness of their shoes on the glossy wooden floor might make somebody mad at them. She pushed down slowly on the bar of the door. Its brassy clunk was as soft as Winna could get it. The door opened with a groan and sighed behind them as if relieved that they had left.

Outside, the sun was bright, reflecting off the cement steps down to the street. She wished she had asked Gramma to order her *two* new pairs of glasses, one to be dark like the pair Benny pulled from his front pocket. He frowned as he put them on. "Legwork take a long time," he said. Like *she* was the one complaining!

They headed up the block, toward the hardware store and the shortcut to Aunt Pic's. She was fixing them lunch. Winna and Benny had disguised their investigation into the doctor's identity and Key's whereabouts as a school project for the fall, a lie her cousin had come up with that Winna felt bad about. Having Benny help her felt like asking the devil, but he hadn't tried to beat her up yet—not so far this morning. And as soon as possible she'd tell his mom the truth. . . .

Winna's thoughts trailed off. There was a second car in Aunt Pic's driveway. They got near and she was sure: this was one she'd never seen before. A midnight-blue Mercury. Visitors? She followed Cousin Benny in through the kitchen door. Voices came through the entrance to the living room, Aunt Pic's and another lady's, someone Winna knew—but where from? Benny was already in there.

"Winna! Your grandparents told me I'd find you here. You're so grown—has it really only been two weeks?—and much more like your mother as a girl without your glasses!" Right on the edge of Aunt Pic's sofa sat Miss Ross, Winna's guidance counselor from Kalamazoo. She put out her arms and gave Winna a quick, light hug. Winna could see she had on a pearly sweater over a polka-dotted dress, and a little hat of feathers like a headband.

Winna liked Miss Ross. When Mom went to high school for one year in Kalamazoo, she'd had her too, which meant Miss Ross was old—old enough to have grey hair—but her eyes sparkled almost all the time because so many things got her excited. And she was tiny, almost as short as a kid, which somehow made up for her being white. She turned to Cousin Benny.

"You must be the man of the house!" Miss Ross always knew the right thing to say. Benny came over and actually smiled. Miss Ross held out her hand and they shook.

"Would you like to have a bite to eat with us?" asked Aunt Pic. "The children are just taking a little lunch break from their studies now."

"Oh, no, I don't want to be a bother. I'm only dropping by. This is my first chance since I heard about Rachel staying so long in the hospital. I just wanted to—studies? In the middle of June? Doesn't the Paw Paw district have the same school calendar we do?"

"You won't be a bother at all—it's only sandwiches." Aunt Pic got up and so did Miss Ross, so everyone wound up in the kitchen together, and it wasn't like having company over. Aunt Pic had made both tuna and egg salad. She opened a jar of pickles from Gramma and cut up carrots and celery into sticks and radishes into roses, and took out an extra loaf of bread, made of rye, from the freezer. It was probably a fancier lunch than what Winna and Benny would have gotten, but they ate it right there instead of in the dining room. Before she sat at her place, Miss Ross remembered she'd bought a bag of potato chips at Hardings on her way to Paw Paw, so she brought them in and they ate those, too.

"Now what is this project about? Something you have to do during summer vacation?" Miss Ross dabbed at her mouth with her napkin and folded it back in her lap. "That seems a pretty strict requirement!"

"Well, it's not," said Winna. "I mean it's not required; it's my own idea." In the seat next to her Benny looked up from his plate like she was trying to steal his food.

"Oh, really? Benny didn't tell me that," Aunt Pic said. She sounded like she wasn't sure who not to believe. "How did you get him to volunteer?"

"We're trying to find out about someone who we're related to." Winna didn't mean to be impolite, but it was easier to kind of ignore Aunt Pic's question and answer Miss Ross.

"Genealogy!" Miss Ross took a big swallow of her iced tea. "That's one of my hobbies! Fascinating, isn't it?"

"Genealogy? Well . . ." Aunt Pic began taking dirty dishes to the sink. "Nothing wrong with that."

Winna jumped up to help her. "And Grampa Carl is telling us what he knows about the olden times." Which he was.

"Wonderful! Winna, Benny, how would you like it if I joined in?"

"That would be cool. Yeah. Cool." Benny nodded his head.

What? Cousin Benny, who hated all his teachers? *He* wanted *Miss Ross* to be part of the investigation?

Winna had planned to go back to the Paw Paw library by herself that afternoon. Then Miss Ross offered to take Winna to Gramma's in Vandalia on her way home to Kalamazoo and Aunt Pic said yes.

The Mercury had a radio, but it was only playing the weather. Miss Ross switched it off so they could talk. "I've been worried about you and Tupelo, Winna, with your mother so sick."

Miss Ross knew everything about everyone. Especially everyone in Winna's family.

"I like you, Winna. You're so smart, and brave, and you care about other people, I can tell. And I care about you."

Winna said thanks.

"I've missed you at school, Winna. Now the year's over my time is free and I'd like to help you in whatever way I can."

"With the genealogy?" A good word to know.

Miss Ross said she had a typewriter and carbon paper and boxes and boxes of envelopes. They were extras from a club she belonged to. She promised she would send letters to every Gonder that Winna found in every phone book of every city where they had bread factories with the name Winna had seen on the sign outside Key's window. Miss Ross didn't even want to know why Winna was picking those certain cities. Benny had been right; it was going to be cool.

If only Mom could be okay till they figured out where Key lived. If only it didn't take too long.

Miss Ross came back Tuesday, the very next day. She had her things ready to set up in Benny's office. She was the perfect size for the table and crate stacks. With the carbon paper she created five copies of every letter she typed, ten times. Benny folded them five at a time, too, making sharp creases in the paper using an empty pop bottle. Winna stuffed the letters in their envelopes and stuck on stamps. This is what they said:

June 12, 1962

Dear (Miss Ross typed in a different first name for every person) Gonder:

I am doing research on our family and I think you are a part of it. My name is Winna Williams and I am going into the Fifth Grade in the fall. My cousin Benjamin Hawkes and my Guidance Counselor Miss Ross are helping.

Here is the question: Do you have a relative named Key Gonder? He is a very old man. He is more than 100 years. He has been missing from our family since he was a little baby. I think you know him and he's your Dad or Uncle or Grandfather or something else.

Please ask him if he wants to come see us. The sooner the better. If I am right I have important information to tell you about his real mother, who is probably not who you think. Her name was Winona and she was my great-great-grandmother.

You can come to Grampa Carl's and Gramma's

house, which is at the address I am sending you this from. They told me it was okay. It is different from what's on the outside of the envelope, which is wrong and crossed out. The right address is at the top of this page. Or if you can come quickly enough Grampa Carl says you are invited to his birthday on June 23. Grampa Carl is turning 75. That isn't terribly old compared to 100 but it is important. The party is also a picnic. It is at Anderson Park near Vandalia, starting at noon.

I look forward to your acquaintance.

Sincerely,
Winna Williams

On Wednesday Grampa Carl drove Winna and Tupelo to the hospital. They brought the swan feather in an envelope Miss Ross had typed the wrong address on. Gramma sent along a round tin with homemade bran muffins inside. The girls split one muffin so the others would fit better. It was sweet and sticky, crammed full of raisins and canned pineapple. Then their hands were too dirty to touch anything. Tupelo tried wiping hers off on her sundress and left smears down both sides. And of course her hands were still a mess.

Winna didn't have to tell; Grampa Carl noticed

for himself at the stoplight on Gull Road. "Bootnose! Leave well enough alone, now—I got some Wet-Naps Dot stowed in the glove box." He parked in the hospital's wide lot under a shade tree and wiped clean their hands and faces, though there was nothing to be done about the dress.

The hospital's outside was romantic and built like a castle, with towers and balconies. Maybe there were statues, too, but Winna's eyes weren't strong enough to see them. The hospital's inside was plain, with tan tiles on the floor and walls that were sort of green. Grampa Carl held both sisters' hands. Winna didn't care if that made her seem babyish. He talked to a white lady, not a nurse, at a desk, and then they went on an elevator to the fifth floor. Other people rode in it with them, but they weren't important. Her clean, damp hands felt colder and colder, and maybe half a muffin had been too much to eat. The elevator gave a little lurch and the door opened and they had to go out. Down the hall. Into a room. Two beds. The first was empty. The second one, near the window, held her mother.

Mom. How long had it been? Weeks. Her eyes were closed and her cheeks looked flat. Her hair stuck to her forehead—it was wet with something.

"Mommy! Wake up!"

"Shhh!" said Winna, but she was glad when Mom's

eyes blinked open and her head turned in their direction. One scrawny hand came out from under the blanket. Like a bird's claw.

But Mom had always been skinny.

"Tupelo? And Winna?" Her words were crow songs. "Why aren't you in school, sugar?"

"It's out for the summer." She should *know* that.

Nobody said anything for a minute. Mom's face turned away to the ceiling.

"We brung you surprises!" Tupelo tugged forward and Grampa Carl came with her. "Muffins! And—"

"Hello, Daddy." Mom's voice sounded like she had found the answer to a hard problem.

"—and I chosed a beautiful feather for you and—"

"How's Mama?" Ignoring Tupelo and talking like her own daughters weren't even there—

Tupelo tore herself loose from Grampa's hand and slammed into Mom's bed so hard it screeched across the linoleum. "Mommy! Mommy! Mommy!" Tupelo was crying, leaning up for a hug from Mom. She had both bird hands out now, patting Tupelo's braids and neck and shoulders, as far as she could reach. And she was crying, too.

Mom was crying.

It was awful. Winna wiped her own eyes as fast as she could, but pretty soon she couldn't see at all. On her face she felt a soft cloth, a handkerchief. Grampa Carl's, she found out, when she was done using it. And Winna was leaning against the bed then, too, and tall enough that she could touch her mom's thin arms, as soft and gentle as possible. Not to hurt her. Not to make her cry more.

Afterward, Grampa Carl took them to Spring Valley Park. They walked dutifully down to the lake and back. Then they went to the eye doctor's and picked up Winna's new replacement glasses that Gramma had called two weeks ago to get made. The same prescription. Their frames were brown and silver. Winna put them on. Nothing was magic.

Out by the highway they stopped at an A&W. No one wanted a hot dog. They all three had root beer floats.

On the drive back to Vandalia Tupelo asked what was wrong with Mom.

"Well, it's the drugs, the medicine they're makin her take that's got her a little mixed up bout what's goin on."

"No, what's *wrong* with her? Why's my mommy sick? When will she be better?"

"Lung problems. She's havin a hard time breathin, bootnose." The answer seemed to satisfy Tupelo. As for *why* Mom had trouble breathing, Winna knew that had to be the Burden of the Coles, no matter what any doctor might say.

Grampa Carl didn't make a prediction of when Mom would be all well again, and Tupelo seemed to forget he owed her one. When they pulled up to the house and Winna let her out, she headed straight inside to use the bathroom.

Winna waited on the front porch for Grampa Carl. He stayed in the truck seat a long time. Finally he opened his door and got out. But then he just stood there. So Winna went over to him.

He wasn't crying, like she'd been afraid of. If she had the spectacles' magic helping her, she'd be able to tell more. Only a week and a half now—

All of a sudden Grampa Carl picked Winna up and threw her in the air and caught her—like she was as little as Tupelo. So strong! He looked old—he *was* old, almost seventy-five! But he carried her over to the porch and up the steps and in the house, hugging her and rubbing his whiskers against her cheeks, smiling all the way.

# Chapter Fifteen

Miss Ross came back to Vandalia on Thursday, which was Flag Day. She had gone to Paw Paw first, but Aunt Pic and Cousin Benny didn't come on the visit with her; they had to go to a meeting for families of dead soldiers.

It was cold and cloudy outside, so everyone sat in the dining room and drank tea. Winna helped by carrying out a plate of banana bread. The condensation on the kitchen windows reminded Winna of how she used to talk with Estelle. Which she missed doing.

The tea tasted very good: Gramma put spices and dried lemon peel in the pot when she made it. Miss Ross had brought a jar of orange blossom honey as a gift and got them to use it right away instead of waiting for a special occasion. It was rich and thick and beautifully golden, but of course Tupelo got it all over her hands and face and Winna had to take her to the bathroom to wash it off.

When they came back, the grown-ups suddenly quit talking. Either they had been discussing secrets about her mom or Winna or Tupelo.

"Now you be sure and come to the party—it'll be Carl's seventy-fifth birthday!" Gramma acted like that was what they'd been talking about.

"Oh, I wouldn't miss it—where is it again?"

"Anderson Park. Noon. June twenty-third. For the family reunion." Gramma was telling her everything, and this was probably the first time.

Miss Ross nodded. "Of course."

Then none of the grown-ups would look at her or one another. Into the quiet Grampa Carl said, "You girls are in luck! I been wantin to tell about me and Dot elopin to Canada and in honor of our guest, here's the story."

## THE RUNAWAYS

*You can easily imagine how strong your gramma struck my fancy when we were courtin, way back in 1911, because she don't look any different now— Dot! I swear it, swear it up and down and on a stack of*

*Bibles! Don't listen to her: I'm the one tellin this—All right, simmer down, now, Dot. At any rate . . .*

*I had seen her around, of course, like I seen her sister, Estelle, but when she turned fifteen, I started to really notice what I was seein. Soon it was Dot this and Dot that: someone would be talkin about cats and I'd have to tell em Dot had two! Yes, I was in love, and I knew by some kinda miracle Dot loved me back.*

*But my mama and daddy wouldn't hear of us gettin married. Dead set against a weddin because of the Burden, which they held Estelle's early passin was on direct account of, and only the latest—*

*Well, I got to tell about the Burden, Dot, or they won't be able to make sense of what I'm sayin. Winna already knows. Fine, then.*

*So for whatever reason my mama and daddy was worried at the way Coles kept gettin killed. Pardon Cole, that was Dot's daddy, he had ten born brothers and sisters besides the one that got lost, Key. Eleven of em born, but only six survived to have babies of their own. Violet drowned, and Swanna, she got accidentally smothered in a haystack in a game. Limber got the whoopin cough, which took off Lincoln and Blessed, too, since they was all sleepin in the same bedroom.*

*And then there was poor little Estelle caught the consumption down in North Carolina. . . . Well, we won't linger on sadness.*

*Now, I wouldn'ta called my own folks superstitious, but I didn't agree with what they'd decided. Dot was the only woman in the world for me, and if she had a Burden it was my job to help her carry it! Soon as I could make my case to Dot, she packed up her grandma's Bible and we set off for Canada.*

*I had a friend with a buggy. No doubt a car woulda been faster, that's right, but didn't anybody I could ask own one. Dot was barely sixteen; we had to lie about her age to get over the border. Crossed at Detroit, same as all them slaves came up outta the South through Vandalia.*

*Somethin about crossin that border seemed to catch the Twins' attention on me more than ever. Or could be it was on account a the marriage. Whatever it— Yes, ma'am, I agree Miss Ross don't wanna hear none a that "hoodoo nonsense," but I only meant to say how our blessins started doublin around then, the horse foalin a pair a fillies and the charity raffle prize you won turnin out worth twice what was advertised and your bumper crop a daffodils overflowin the window box— But they is facts, Dot!*

*No, Winna, we weren't wedded in a church, but*

*an office. No, they didn't throw rice or tie shoes to the buggy—nobody in Ontario knew us. The window box—jam-packed with flowers—was set out on the south side a this house on a farm where we lived for a couple months after the weddin—wanted to make certain couldn't nobody split us up. We weren't plannin to show our faces back here again till we were good and married in the eyes of the law and man.*

*When we finally did come home, it was because Dot's daddy, Pardon, had taken sick. He was real ill. Died, in fact—pneumonia. Lungs filled up with— Oh, yes ma'am, I got them family trees we mentioned upstairs—I'll just run up right quick and fetch em down for you to take a look.*

Grampa Carl crossed the hall to the bedroom and Winna heard the stair closet open. His footsteps clomped above the ceiling, headed for his altar, but when he came back all he carried were rolled-together sheets of paper. No branches. The papers were the trees. The lines drawn on them were like limbs, and the oldest, first family members were the trees' trunks. The one for Grampa Carl began with John Hawkes. Born 1833. Died 1885. Married in 1860 to Rutha Taber Hawkes—was she the one who made friends with an otter spirit? Yes.

Grampa Carl knew exactly where Great-Great-Grandmother Winona was hiding in Tennessee when she had Key—he had said when he told them Winona's Tale.

"Little settlement called Garland over near Memphis, only a couple miles east of the Mississippi," he told Winna when she asked him again. "Miz Rachel always sent that family a Christmas ham or a bottle of cordial or *somethin* every year, till finally by the time I turned fourteen all the parcels begun comin back marked 'Addressee Unknown.'"

If you knew stories to go with every name and date, like Grampa Carl did, family trees might be interesting. But she didn't see any more clues about lifting the Burden. Plus Tupelo wasn't allowed to touch the rolls of paper or to have more than three slices of banana bread, so pretty soon Winna had to take her to put on a sweater and go outside. At least it wasn't raining.

They played "Ding-Dong Delivery." This was a game Tupelo had made up herself. The idea was that a mysterious package got delivered to one kid, who then tried to guess what was in it by its size, shape, et cetera. Since the package was always another kid, wrapped up in a blanket or something, the ending was, as Benny put it, "stale."

The only good thing was that outside, Winna could

see down the driveway to the mailbox. When the postman came she'd be there before anyone.

Probably it was too soon for her letters to get an answer. The truck drove up and left some envelopes in the box and she raced Tupelo there anyway. Winna won, but she let her little sister beat her back to the house. She stopped on the porch steps to peek at the names and addresses. Nothing from anyone named Gonder. Nothing for her.

Gramma was in the kitchen running water for dishes. Grampa Carl and Miss Ross were just leaving the dining room; the family trees were rolled up again and stuck under Grampa Carl's arm. "Thank you, bootnose," he said as she handed him the mail. "Though I don't mind the walk up to the road . . . but that's right, you're expectin somethin."

He shuffled through the short pile. "Buncha bills." He gave Miss Ross a worried look. "Tupelo, you wanna help open these? Winna, show Miss Ross to her car for me."

Miss Ross had parked under the crabapple, next to Grampa Carl's truck. She opened up the Mercury's front passenger door. "Come sit inside here with me a moment out of the wind, Winna. I have an offer to make." Winna got in.

Clear, bumpy plastic covered the seats' blue fabric.

Miss Ross put her purse in the back and sat on a cushion on the driver's side. She laid one arm against the steering wheel. "I have an idea of how to help you with a big problem. But it's one you haven't thought about yet. I don't mean to discourage you, Winna, but . . ." She stopped talking.

"But what?" The car was cold. The plastic crackled as Winna put her hands under her legs. After that it was quiet again.

Finally Miss Ross finished her sentence. ". . . but how do you know the name of this relative you're searching for?"

"From Grampa Carl. Like I told you. It's not made up—"

"No, of course not. But—but this old relative—"

"Key. Key Gonder." She had told Miss Ross that, and besides, it was in all the letters.

"Yes, Winna, you're going by what his mother called him, but whoever took him from her, they would have adopted him; he'd be going by their last name for sure, and most likely he'd use a different first name as well. Winna? Winna, don't cry now. . . ."

Why not? Why shouldn't she cry? It was all wasted, the typing and the letters and the stamps and none of it was going to do any good! The lost baby, Key—the old man in the wheelchair—was still alive, but he could be called anything! She opened the door to leave, but where could she go? Nowhere was safe. Her mom was in the hospital dying like Estelle had died, like Violet and Swanna and Limber and all the rest, slain by the Burden of the Coles and Winna couldn't do anything, not even hide from it—

"Shut the door, Winna. And don't give up. Remember, I promised to help." Miss Ross was saying the same thing Mom and now Winna always said. Had Mom got the idea from Miss Ross in the first place, when she had Miss Ross for a school counselor too?

Don't give up. Well, Winna wanted to. Really, really— She closed the car door softly. Her tears and sobbing steamed up the window. No words appeared.

Miss Ross had a good idea. She belonged to a gene-alogy club with members all over the country. She would put Winona's Tale in their monthly newsletter that got mailed out next Monday. Someone who knew something would see it and write them to say where Key was and what was his new name.

She really liked Winna's suggestion about finding the doctor's name using the same method, and said one way or another they would figure things out. It was good to know he had probably lived in Garland.

Winna huddled in her sweater and wiped her dumb tears off with the ends of her sleeves. Miss Ross drove around to the front of the house and dropped her off. Winna nodded yes when she asked if she should mail a copy of the newsletter to Gramma and Grampa Carl's address. Before going back in the house she stood by herself outside for a few minutes to let the wind finish drying her face.

Putting Winona's Tale in a national newsletter was a good idea. A great idea. It would work. Almost for sure—especially if they found the doctor's name, too.

And almost for sure it would take too long.

# Chapter Sixteen

Hot wind puffed the damp sheets into fat bellies, pushed them up along the backyard clothesline where they were pinned. Winna was tall enough to hang them herself without Gramma's help. By the time she finished the last clean pillowcase in the basket, the curtains she'd done first were nearly dry. They could all come down before Tupelo woke up from her nap.

Winna was still being good. As if that might make a difference in what happened to her mom.

The sun shone almost directly above her head. Time for the mail truck to come.

Today it had been a week since they sent off the letters Miss Ross typed. Tomorrow it would be a week since they saw Mom, though Winna and Tupelo had gotten to talk to her on the telephone every night after supper. She seemed to talk for shorter and shorter times.

Winna walked around the west side of the house, passing under the crabapple. She felt like its leaves: moving around, but dusty and hopeless.

Not a single answer had come so far to even one of Winna's fifty letters. The only things the mailman had brought Winna were some of those same letters back—the post office was returning them because the addresses where she sent them didn't work.

Yesterday Gramma and Grampa Carl had shared their copy of Miss Ross's newsletter with her. Winona's Tale was on the second page. A lady reporter had seen the newsletter and called this afternoon to ask more about it. She wanted to write a feature article for *The Paw Paw Courier*. The lady was someone Winna had never heard of: Mrs. Tate. Maybe if she could get Walter Cronkite to broadcast it as news on TV that would bring results soon enough.

Winna reached the mailbox. The truck had already left—she heard its motor going farther and farther down the road. She reached inside the hot metal box. Here were a bunch of envelopes: some for bills, with windows cut out of them or printed labels; two big mint-green envelopes and an extra-long blue one, all for Mr. Carl

Hawkes, which Winna figured had to be birthday cards; and a very ordinary envelope from Truman Gonder, Esq. in Portland, Oregon.

Her answer.

Miss Ross had been wrong. The baby's name had stayed the same and been recognized.

Winna stared at the envelope in her hand, letting her feet guide her back toward the house. She hardly saw the steps as she climbed them to the porch. She sat on the glider and opened the ordinary envelope that would save her mother's life. The letter was in cursive. The words were squeezed close together to each other on the page.

First Truman Gonder's name again and his address again, on Malt—Multi—Multnomah Street. Then came the date he wrote it: June 15, 1962. Last Friday. In a few minutes Winna had read the rest:

Miss Winna Williams:

I thank you for your kind letter of June 12 regarding Mr. Key Gonder. As you guessed, we are indeed your relatives. I and my sister, Mrs. Eleanora Gonder Forsythe, were much pleased to hear from you.

My father, Dwayne Gonder, Grandfather Key's son, is now deceased, as is my father's mother, Rebecca

Gonder, née Gilkie (of the Garland Gilkies), who was Grandfather Key's wife. So, alas, is our own dear mother, Katherine, and Mr. Charles Forsythe, my sister's husband. Fortunately they did have a child, Mr. Charles Forsythe, Jr., currently stationed in Germany.

Grandfather Key, as you will be glad to know, is still alive and very, very well for someone of such an advanced age.

Depending on certain circumstances, my sister and I may be able to accept your invitation to Grampa Carl's birthday picnic as a preamble to our upcoming vacation, for there are other relatives in Paw Paw we could visit at the same time. We hope that a telegram will be an acceptable method of letting you know if this last-minute change of plans turns out to be possible, as you have not provided us with your phone number.

However, I fear that strong as he is, there is no chance that Grandfather Key will be included in our visit to you. Perhaps, if all goes well, he can come with us to see you at a later date. Grandfather Key is confined to a wheelchair in a nursing home, and we would rather not risk having him travel so far on such short notice.

Sincerely yours,
Truman Gonder, Esquire

It was over. Winna sat quietly smiling to herself. She forgot about the laundry drying on the line in the backyard and simply sat where she was. She didn't have to try so hard to be good anymore.

She should have put in Grampa Carl and Gramma's phone number even though it was unlisted, and even if it was long distance—but that didn't make any difference because now Key was found. The Burden of the Coles was lifted.

Mom was safe.

"Winna!" Gramma's call interrupted the soft nothingness of her thoughts.

"Coming, Gramma!" She stood up and folded her letter, remembering to pick up the other envelopes and carry them in to the living room table on her way to the kitchen.

Gramma was actually in the pantry with the door to the backyard open. The sheets billowed beyond her, obviously dry, but Gramma was stooping to reach some pots of plants on the steps. "Wake your sister up. You and her can ride to Picquetta's with Grampa Carl when he gets home from the barber's and take her these rosemaries he dug up for her. Then she got a surprise for you he's supposed to bring back over here in the truck."

Good. She could tell Benny and thank him for his legwork. But what surprise?

Winna lay down next to Tupelo on the hide-a-bed. Had she saved her little sister from the Burden as well as her mom? She would never need to know. She tickled Tupelo under one pleasingly plump arm, which was kind of a chancy thing to do while she was asleep, but it only made her giggle and get up quick and go to the bathroom.

Grampa Carl returned from the barber's with his hair a little shorter and a lot darker. Gramma put the pots of rosemarys on the floor between Winna's feet. They drove off on gravel. Stones ticked against the bottom of the truck. Then they got to the blacktop. It was eight miles to Paw Paw. She knew the way after going back and forth so many times. If it wasn't so far she could have walked it.

Tupelo had to pee again as soon as they arrived in Paw Paw. While Aunt Pic hurried her to the bathroom, Grampa Carl and Winna carried the plant pots in and put them in the empty kitchen sink. Benny wasn't around.

"Seem like you musta got good news today," Grampa Carl said.

Of course she should have told him! This was the first time they were alone. That was an excuse. Winna handed him the letter she was keeping folded in her shorts' back pocket.

Another harrumphing noise like when he didn't tell

her Mom was so sick. "Ain't that amazin! Key Gonder found! After all these years . . . I expect they'll be lettin your mama outta the hospital real soon—maybe next week!" He nodded, then frowned. "Won't be needin them specs repaired, then?"

Winna couldn't imagine not saying goodbye to Estelle. "Would that still be okay?" She was only going to have to wait a couple more days now. "Unless it's too much work?"

"Naw, all that's been done taken care of. I'll have em ready by Saturday without extra hoodooin. Besides, you never know."

"Never know what?"

Before he could answer, Aunt Pic and Tupelo came out of the bathroom. Tupelo was waving her wet hands in the air. "Ready for the surprise now!" They trooped out the door to the garage.

It was a blue Lady Schwinn. Big enough for a grown-up, with a headlight and a handlebar basket and one basket more on each side of the back wheel. Aunt Pic was giving the bicycle to Winna as a present, since she never used it these days.

"Wow!" This bike was way bigger than her one in Kalamazoo. Winna stood on the pedals and coasted down to the street, then rode back up the driveway. Only Grampa Carl and Tupelo were still standing there.

Actually, Tupelo was sitting down on the ground crying. She stopped long enough to ask, "Why don't I get nuffin? I been good, too!"

"Yes, you have," said Aunt Pic, emerging from the darkness at the garage's back. "Winna knows that, so she'll be giving you lots of rides on her back seat. It's really almost a bike for the both of you"—Aunt Pic winked at Winna—"but I got you your own gift anyway, since you *are* so little." She set down the wooden box she'd been carrying. "I made some 3-D puzzles for Benny a few years back. People might think you're pretty young to work these, but—"

"Let me see!" Tupelo demanded. Winna looked, too. The puzzles were painted wood shaped like bananas and apples and cups and bells—not flat, though, but round, with pegs sticking out and holes where those pegs would fit. Tupelo grabbed a couple and matched them together. They looked right. She kept playing while Aunt Pic lowered the Lady Schwinn's seat a few inches. Testing it out again, determined not to wobble so much, Winna rode to the corner and saw Cousin Benny coming home. She braked and showed him Truman Gonder, Esquire's letter.

"Foun the victim? Perpetrator's probly dead by this time. Statue of limitations." Cousin Benny nodded wisely and continued homeward. Winna made sure to stay behind his miniwheel all the way back. The driveway was empty when they got there. Winna heard Tupelo and Grampa Carl's voices in the kitchen. She had to think of a name for her new bike. She leaned it on its kickstand and climbed the concrete steps.

"Hey! Where you goin? We need to close the case file!" Cousin Benny motioned her to follow him into his office. Then he wanted her to give him her letter. She didn't fight him, but she was glad he made her a copy of it to take home. She put the page from his notebook in her pocket.

With an important expression on his face, he opened the drawer and put the letter inside and shut it with both hands. He turned around and nodded at Winna again. "Another case solved thanks to good, old-fashioned legwork."

Thanks to typing and licking envelopes, too, Winna thought, remembering Miss Ross's work. And her own. But what she said was, "And all because of you!"

Cousin Benny pursed his lips and tilted his head to the side like he was considering if she had said something right. Two more nods. "You deserve the credit for askin me." He turned out the light. "Ima keep that in mind, next mystery I find needs solvin."

Aunt Pic had given Grampa Carl and Tupelo ice cream to eat. She got bowls out for Winna and Cousin

Benny when they came in. Only Black Walnut, but it was cold and sweet.

Grampa Carl had already finished his serving. He leaned back in his chair and wiped his mouth with his handkerchief. "What do you say we telephone your mama early, bootnoses, on account of"—he looked sideways at Winna—"on account of it's a special day." Aunt Pic's phone had an extra-long cord; it reached all the way to the kitchen table. The children ate quietly while Grampa Carl called the hospital and asked for Mrs. Williams.

"What's that you're sayin?" he asked the receiver. "What?" He stopped smiling. "You sure? Couldn't be a mistake—*Rachel* Williams?" He stood up from the table and walked out of the room, still talking. Winna didn't even know she was following him till Aunt Pic put her hand on Winna's shoulder and guided her back to her chair.

By the time Grampa Carl came in again with the phone hung up, her ice cream had melted. It was only Black Walnut, anyway.

"The hospital moved Rachel to Intensive Care," Grampa Carl told Aunt Pic. "Can't nobody talk to her or see her. Seems like she's had a turn for the worse."

# Chapter Seventeen

Cousin Benny's idea was to go to the graveyard at midnight or some creepy time like that. "But we won't be able to *see* anything," Winna told him as she helped him tuck in a blanket on the living room sofa. She and Tupelo were sleeping over at Aunt Pic's so Grampa Carl and Gramma could drive to the hospital. Just so they would be there and able to see Mom as soon as the doctors said.

At least Winna got to have her own place on the couch. Let Aunt Pic worry about getting wet on by baby Tupelo. She stuffed a round cushion in a pillowcase and tossed it on the end of the couch where her head would go. Done.

"We can take flashlights," Cousin Benny decided. He

really only wanted to do something weird and exciting. It wasn't *his* mother in Intensive Care, so sick she might die. *Winna* wanted to do something, too—but something that would make a difference. So she had to visit Covey Hill to talk to Great-Great-Grandmother Winona, like she'd let slip. She had to find out why the Burden wasn't lifted. Sure. But not at night. And not without being able to see and talk to ghosts. Which Benny didn't believe in.

If the specs got powerful-er the way fruit got riper, a little at a time, in the morning she'd be one day closer to seeing ghosts again. Maybe it would be like *Magic or Not* and the specs would at least sort of work. If she could put Benny off till then—if her mom could live that long—

"Midnight's too early," she said. That was a last-minute strategy. Negotiating. And surprisingly, Benny accepted she was right.

"Yeah, too risky." He nodded. "It's summer, and stayin light till nine, nearly ten. People might still be up by midnight. I come get you around two."

Winna made a kind of mmm-hmm-ish sound and moved her head so it sort of could look like a nod yes. She would pretend to be so deep asleep she was practically in a coma. Just let him try to wake her up without ruining his plan by making too much noise.

Once Aunt Pic turned off the lamp and closed her bedroom door to a crack, though, Winna knew she would never fall truly asleep. She made herself lie on the couch like a log, stone-still except the fingers of one hand rubbing over the vine-and-leaf patterns cut into the couch's furry back. Which was worse? Stumbling around in a pitch-black graveyard full of invisible ghosts or having Mom turn into one? Asking that question was a waste of time, but what else did she have to think about?

She hadn't brought her pajamas, which meant her underwear was already on. Blouse and jeans folded on the couch's far arm. Ready and waiting. And waiting.

Finally, *finally*, she heard the creak and click of Aunt Pic's door pushed all the way shut. A moment later, Cousin Benny appeared, green and spooky in the bathroom's nightlight. He grabbed her by a shoulder and she shook him off and jumped up to show she wasn't even slightly sleeping. Then she got her clothes on quickly to cover up her drawers. It was okay—Cousin Benny was related—but Winna felt better after she was dressed. Then they tiptoed through the kitchen to the garage for their bikes.

On the way she noticed the stove said it was later than she would have thought: five after four in the morning! Maybe she had only dreamed that she stayed up?

Benny said he would take them on a secret shortcut, a path that went to Covey Hill faster than the regular highway. "Dawn Patrol!" Cousin Benny shouted when they were far enough from the town. "I'm Sherlock Holmes!"

"Who am I?"

"Robin Hood!"

Fine. She liked playing she lived in the forest and shot arrows. But what did that have to do with Sherlock Holmes and bicycles? At least Benny was enjoying himself.

The ride would actually have been sort of fun if she wasn't so worried. They went between bushes along hidden trails. The grass brushed her ankles with dew. Nobody saw them, but Winna could tell other people were up, too—well, this was the country. Winna heard horses neighing and roosters crowing and pigs grunting and men and women yelling at their animals.

The sky was already a thin blue color like paintbrush water. Realistically it would be at least five o'clock by the time they reached Covey Hill. Sunrise. Then what? Was Benny going to pretend they were still in the dark?

The hill started and Winna stood on her pedals to keep going. Around and around and up and up and up. It was hard, sweaty work. At last they reached the top. The iron gates were open, but Winna went to the stone pillars where they hung from and knocked the way she remembered Grampa Carl doing.

"You ain't comin in." That was Cousin Benny's voice—but was it also a dead person telling Winna to stay out?

"Whatsa matter? Chicken?" Benny already stood inside the cemetery's walls. He had put his hands inside his back pockets so his elbows stuck out at angles. "Girls always too scared to do anythin, even in the daylight."

"No I am not!" Winna walked toward him in big, determined steps, swinging her arms . . . and stopped. Why did the air feel so suddenly cold around her? The direct opposite of when she had held Estelle's hand?

She could go ahead anyway. Nothing was keeping her from doing what she wanted . . . but what did she really want to do? Right now she could tell Estelle and Great-Great-Grandmother Winona everything. But since she didn't have the specs, she'd never get their answers to any of her important questions.

She should come back later. With the spectacles. By herself.

"Wait a minute. I need to check on—"

"Uh-huh! Scaredy-cat *girl*—you ain't checkin on nothin and nobody!" Cousin Benny's fake laugh sounded even meaner than his real one. He spat at the ground and turned his back. "I ain't waitin. *You* wait!

Wait right here while I explore all through this place, because I ain't one little bit afraid of it!"

Well, of course she wasn't going to wait there for him to come back and call her names. Winna brought her bike to where she could coast back down the bumpy dirt road. There really *was* something she wanted to check on: when Grampa Carl drove them here, and also this morning, she had seen an interesting-looking path going off from the right side of the road. Could she spot it coming from this direction?

Yes. Two circles below the cemetery, she saw a tall tree covered in flowers that was halfway hiding a tunnel of leftover night. She parked and walked under its drooping branches, which this close she realized were just regular oak or something with another plant, one with pink roses, wrapped around it.

The path was made of stones, which must be why it even still existed. Winna didn't think anyone had been on it in a long while. Daylight was shining ahead, so she kept going forward, step by step. Cousin Benny ought to see her now: she was a hero of courage.

When she got to the lighter area at the path's end, there was a wide hole in the earth, like a big sandbox. On the far side stood a naked wall with two empty windows in its middle, left over from when some old house fell into ruin. The windows' tops arched up like eyebrows. Winna wanted to look out of them. She jumped down into the hole, which was filled with weeds and humps of dirt and rocks, and climbed to where the windows opened.

They were higher than she could reach to grab onto their sides and pull herself up. She had to crane her neck back, and even then all she saw was a bush waving leaf tips and a butterfly flitting back and forth and birds looping loop after loop and clouds scooting around in the wind as if they were swimming swans. But she could smell delicious delight! Lilies and daisies, hollyhocks and honeysuckles . . . a whole garden, and only inches away—she had to get there! If only she had wings, if only she could fly the way those little acrobatic birds did . . . but they'd gone someplace else, now, somewhere out of sight—

Suddenly the twittering songs of other birds came loudly to her ears. Why had it been so quiet before? Was she waking up? Had she gone to sleep? She heard shouting—her name. Cousin Benny was calling her.

"Winna! I'm goin! Where you at? Get your butt—" She couldn't tell the rest of his words. She walked fast back to the road. The path seemed shorter now, and much less frightening. Lots lighter. Her bike was where she'd left it. The handlebars were hot!

Cousin Benny pushed off down the spiraling road

as soon as she sat on her seat. She was mostly able to keep up.

At the hill's bottom he took the turn away from the church to the highway. They didn't need to be so fast now. As they came to the highway's big curve toward Paw Paw, a huge dog ran toward her out of the shadows of a driveway's trees, barking and growling. Winna tried to ride faster and catch up with her cousin, but that made her bike wobble so hard she fell off. "ROWFF! WUFF! GRRRRRR!" Snapping and snarling, the furious dog put both front paws on top of the tiny fence barely keeping it in. It barked louder, meaner. The thing was going to get out. Winna pulled her bike up from the gravel and stood it between her and the dangerous animal.

"Sport! Down, Sport!" a kid's voice shouted. A boy walked up the driveway with his hands in his pockets—it was Tony from school, Marcus's twin. The dog kept barking, but a little quieter. It jumped off the fence and began running back and forth beside it.

Before he reached the fence, Tony stopped. "Hey, it's the giraffe! What are you doing out of the jungle?" he asked her.

"Me?"

"Ridin her bike down a public street—what it look like?" Cousin Benny skidded his tires sideways and hopped to the ground. "What you doin?"

A screen door twanged open and Marcus joined Tony under the sunrise sky. "You ain't welcome here, *boy*," he said, folding his arms and frowning.

Benny had dropped his vee-barred, banana-seated treasure in the dirt as if it were nothing. He was walking straight at the boys in stiff steps like a gunslinger. The dog, Sport, backed up to a crouch but barked faster and higher like a maniac.

Cousin Benny was only inches away now from the bullies. He stood up tall and yelled:

**"I ain't no 'boy' cause I'm fully-growed!**
**If I'm ever a *boy* I'll *tell* you so!"**

Then he put both hands into fists, ready to punch them right in their noses.

"Children!" A woman ran out of the shadowy house. Miss Tooma? No; her hair was shorter and curlier and her cheeks more puffy and pink. "What have I told you about mixing with coloreds outside of school! Don't touch them—they could have germs!"

"Who you callin a germ?" Cousin Benny asked.

Miss Tooma's lookalike ignored him. "Sport! Heel!" she ordered. The dog shut up and slunk behind her. "Now get in the house, you two! Morning chores! The reservoir on the new range holds ten gallons of water— that's two buckets each you need to pump."

Winna thought fast. The reporter she talked to

yesterday about Winona's Tale had been called Mrs. Tate. Marcus and Tony's last name was Tate, and this lady was acting as if she was their mother. Hoping she sounded like Mom, she stuck out her hand and said, "I believe we spoke on the phone yesterday? I'm Winna Williams."

The lady looked at her. She didn't reach over the fence to shake, only wiped her palms on her apron like they itched. Her blue eyes squinted down and she twitched her head in a tiny "No" motion. Then her mouth puckered like she was going to spit. But its corners pointed up, so she was probably supposed to be smiling. "What a surprise! Despite that piece in the newsletter, I had the distinct impression over the telephone—I told my sons they must be mistaken when they said you were a—You're so articulate! Such a good vocabulary!"

Sometimes being nice took work. But at least Mrs. Tate was trying.

"Would you like to come sit . . . on the porch?" the woman asked.

"Why?" Benny asked. His arms were hanging at his sides again, but his hands still bunched themselves into fists.

Miss Tooma's lookalike got taller. "And who might you be?"

"My cousin, Benny," Winna explained, but Mrs. Tate kept talking only to Winna.

"I ought to interview you in a bit more depth, and it will be much easier in person . . . and before I get too involved in the day. I'll contact your parents later for verification and further follow-up—"

"My daddy dead," Benny interrupted. "Inna service to his country." Marcus giggled. Why was that funny?

Winna explained about her parents' divorce and her mom being in the hospital as Mrs. Tate opened the gate and invited her up to the house's porch. Sport whined and barked and jerked his collar, but Tony had a good hold on it. So Winna acted brave and walked right past without flinching.

The sun had been completely up for a long while. Mrs. Tate wanted to call Aunt Pic and say where they were, and Winna felt guilty for that not being her own idea.

"Nah, it's cool," said Benny. "I left her a note on my bed sayin me and Winna was out investigatin and would be back before lunchtime." She should have thought of that, too.

Mrs. Tate sat down on a wicker couch with a pen and a pad of paper and sent her sons to fill the reservoir and then to weed the garden before it got too hot. "And tell your aunt we need some juice from the kitchen on your way out. Three servings."

The aunt who came carrying the juice and said hello was the real Miss Tooma. She and Mrs. Tate were twin sisters. That explained how they looked so much the same. Twins ran in families. A baby started to cry inside the house. Miss Tooma set down her tray of Dixie cups and went back in and the crying stopped. The juice was grapefruit. Winna sipped slowly, glad the cup was so small. Benny sat next to her on a big, square-cushioned stool Mrs. Tate called an ottoman. Twice, so that must really be what it was.

Though as a reporter Mrs. Tate asked the most questions, Winna found out things herself, such as Mrs. Tate's first name, which Winna would of course never use. But it was Claire. And she called Miss Tooma Beverly. And the baby was nearly three years old, and her name was Cressida.

But the hugest revelation of all was the picture.

After going over Winona's Tale *again* and this time adding the name of the town near where the baby got lost—or stolen—Winna felt so thirsty she wished she still had some grapefruit juice left. But it would be rude to hint she wanted more. Anyway, Miss Tooma, who would probably have to bring it again, had suddenly gone back inside to look for something.

"I gotta pee," Cousin Benny announced. He stood up and headed for the door inside.

"Marcus! Tony!" shouted Mrs. Tate. She had a loud voice. "Show our guest the outhouse!"

As soon as Benny said anything, Winna had to go too. But she could wait for a place with indoor plumbing.

The twins both came to the front steps, like it would take two of them to do what their mom told them. Their skin was red and sweaty. They grinned and giggled as they walked off toward the back with Cousin Benny.

Miss Tooma returned with a brown leather book and set it on the ottoman. "Since you mentioned Garland, I thought you'd like to see this. Mr. Tate's father, Aurelius, was born and raised there, and his mother too, before they married and followed the North Star Highway up here."

Winna's hands were clean—cleaner than Marcus's and Tony's, anyway—but Mrs. Tate didn't want her to touch the book, which was a "private, limited addition." She made a face at Miss Tooma for bringing it out, but then she seemed so proud of it she decided to turn the pages herself so Winna could look.

On the second page in was the doctor.

Not in color, and way older. But it was still an unmistakable photograph of *him*—the same man the spectacles had shown taking away Key.

"Stop." Without thinking, Winna put her hand on Mrs. Tate's arm to keep her from turning further. The reporter lady shook her arm like a fly had landed on it. Winna realized she should have said "please." "I'm sorry." The little words printed at the page's bottom were hard to read from where she sat. "Who's that?" She got up to see better.

Mrs. Tate pulled the book away. "That's Mr. Tate's grandfather. Dr. Louis Kenneth Gilkie." Winna remembered the name "Gilkie" from Truman Gonder, Esquire's letter. The doctor was the father of Key's wife, Rebecca. These white people must be part of her family.

Other photos in the book proved it: baby pictures of Truman and Eleanora, his sister. And one showed a lady leaning against a man who *had* to be Key, but the printing below spelled a name Winna had never heard before: Elihu. But surely he must be Great-Great-Grandmother Winona's lost baby, whom Winna had seen as an old man living near a bread factory. She got a good long look at him, too, because Miss Tooma made Mrs. Tate keep the page open. Key's face—all the Gonders' faces—had that same look as Gramma's: soft and round like apple dumplings.

Miss Tooma sighed and folded her hands together. "So romantic!"

"Romantic piffle!" Mrs. Tate made the same face she'd made when Miss Tooma came out with the book.

"A childless marriage may have been the reason the Gilkies adopted little Elihu, but once that trouble ended and they had their own offspring, it was only out of the goodness of Doctor Gilkie's heart those two were raised as brother and sister. And then to let his real daughter marry that Elihu! Such a scandal! All that was Elihu's fault; simply moving out West and changing his name didn't clear up the mess. I wonder if the Gilkies ever forgave him.

"And they say he had Indian blood in him—or worse!" She glared at Winna—who had apologized!

No use trying to kid herself any longer. Though she hadn't used any bad words, Mrs. Tate was as prejudiced against Negroes as her sons were. Maybe more. She hadn't even let Winna or Benny in the house. Winna felt relieved of having to stay.

"Thank you for the drinks. They were very"—she wasn't going to lie—"refreshing. We'll be going now." Winna climbed down the steps and out into the bright morning.

From where the driveway went around the side of the house she heard Benny's voice, low and mean: "Get your cracka hands off my seat!"

# Chapter Eighteen

"I was only moving it away from the road!" Tony had Benny's bike, rolling it up the driveway by the handlebars and banana seat. Marcus had Winna's the same way. They were probably telling the truth, but Benny stood wide-legged right in front of them, stopping them where no grown-ups could see.

"Anything you do to my bike Ima do to you," said Benny. "I swear."

"Swear? On your grandmother's grave?" Making kissing noises, Tony leaned over with his tongue out, getting ready to lick the seat's shiny leopard covering.

"My gramma ain't dead. But *you* is." He grabbed his bike and shoved it toward Winna. "Hold this while I kill me a couple peckerwoods."

Another fight! What would Aunt Pic say? Or worse, Mom in Intensive Care—she shouldn't have to worry about bad stuff happening! And even if Winna and Benny beat these two bullies now, the war between them could keep going on and on and on. . . . Winna had to do something or say something, anything—

"Listen!" She shoved the bike against the house wall. "I found out an important clue in there. Benny! Benny!" She caught her cousin's arm. "They're our cousins or somebody like that—through the perpetrator! We're *related*!"

"You a story!" Benny tore loose and twisted around to face her. "Ain't neither!"

Marcus yelled at her, too, and pushed her bike at her so hard she had to press herself against the house's white boards to not fall down. Tony's mouth opened and shut twice without any words coming out. Then he began cursing. Sam and Ken were running up the driveway—where had they come from? Things were getting worse, not better.

The grown-ups couldn't see them but they heard the noise. Mrs. Tate came around from the front, followed by Miss Tooma holding Cressida, who was crying. Winna had a hard time explaining what she'd said when she tried to end the first argument and started this second, bigger one. Because no one wanted to understand or believe her.

Only Mrs. Tate, who Winna could tell didn't enjoy thinking about being related to Negroes, listened to the whole story—probably because she was a reporter and used to doing that. But it was also probably why she asked so many questions. Winna answered with the facts about almost everything except how she had recognized the doctor, Louis Gilkie. She wasn't dumb enough to say with magic. Even Cousin Benny, another kid, would call her crazy.

"I got a letter from Mr. Gonder. Mr. Truman Gonder." Not a lie. "In Oregon. He's my—" Had she figured that part out yet? "—my great-uncle's grandson. And he's in your book."

Mrs. Tate turned red and white at the same time and looked again at Miss Tooma, a look so mean Winna felt sorry for her. "A connection we're not proud of, and by marriage—and a rather dubious marriage at that."

What was the definition of dubious? Sort of fake, according to what she remembered. What would make a marriage fake?

"May I see your 'letter'?" Mrs. Tate held out her hand.

"I didn't bring it."

"Of course you didn't." This time Mrs. Tate's smile took up the whole bottom of her face. She straightened up from bending over and reaching.

"But I brought a copy." Winna still had it in her pants

190

pocket from yesterday. She pulled it out, the proof. Mrs. Tate took the folded page from Benny's notebook by its corners and opened it. Her smile stayed wide.

"Very creative. Very imaginative."

You didn't hit grown-ups. Even prejudiced ones. "It's real. Not a story." As quickly as she could, Winna took the copy back. Mrs. Tate wasn't holding it so tight. "Thank you. We won't keep you any longer." She wanted to sound polite, like a kid in a book.

Ken and Sam and Marcus and Tony were in her way. She stuffed the copy back in her pocket and steered her bike toward the driveway's end as if they weren't there, and they moved. From way behind her the dog Sport began barking strangled-sounding barks. It must be tied up. She would ignore it.

She reached the street. She was not going to give up. Not after that almost-fight. She had to lift the Burden.

Should she go to Vandalia now instead of to Aunt Pic's and take the specs from Grampa Carl's altar? Even though they weren't quite ready? If you opened the oven door too soon on cupcakes and banged it shut, they fell flat instead of rising. And tasted gummy and bad like that batch Tupelo had wrecked at Easter.

She could take the specs and go back to Covey Hill on her own and see if this time she got in. That would show she wasn't scared.

Here came Cousin Benny, biking down the dusty gravel, skidding to a stop. "Dumb bullies," he said. "I made em promise they was gonna come play on my team at the reunion picnic when they get proved they wrong."

"You believe me about us being in the same family after all?" Winna asked.

"Yeah. You my cousin. But they your dumb relatives, not mine." Which made no sense, but Benny seemed satisfied, so she didn't say anything back. He took off again, pedaling onto the road and turning left, toward the highway, the way they had been going. "Come on!"

Winna caught up but stayed behind him. She stopped at the turnoff to Grampa Carl's and Gramma's, and for a moment she thought he noticed. He yelled over his shoulder for her to come on. But she stayed put till he was out of sight. Till a grasshopper crossed the highway, it was so deserted. Then she was sure.

She rode away on her own. Aunt Pic would be mad when Cousin Benny came home without her. Winna would have to make up some excuse. That was a problem, but maybe the spectacles could help her with it.

When she got to the house, though, she realized she had a much bigger problem. Grampa Carl's truck was parked in front. He had come back already from the hospital.

Now she needed to do everything sneakily, and it would feel exactly like what it was: stealing.

She was not giving up. She was going to be a robber. A thief.

She was doing it to save Mom.

Winna tiptoed across the porch and opened up the front door as quietly as she could. Nobody in the living room. The hallway was empty, too. She peeked in the kitchen. Nobody. Were Grampa Carl and Gramma in the bathroom? They wouldn't both be in there at the same time, and the bedroom with the hidden stairs was the other direction, so that was the way she went. The dining room had no one in it, as usual.

The pretend closet's door stood a little ways open, spilling dim, golden light. Maybe sunshine getting in? She went up. No. The golden light was candles—a pair of them. Against their glow she saw Grampa Carl as a tall shadow, moving, bending, turning to one side, then another. Talking to himself in a low whisper Winna barely heard. If he hadn't seen her yet, she could leave—

"Come on, Winna, and give me a hand here. This'll be a lot more use with you helpin."

"Okay." She climbed the rest of the way and went toward the light. And suddenly she felt better. By the candles she could see Grampa Carl's face, tireder and wrinklier than ever before. But not as grey and worried as last night. That had to mean Mom was better.

"Rachel appears to have turned a corner. Now I'm hopin to keep her on the right side of it." Grampa Carl waved at a towel lying on the carpet. A glass of water and the two burning candles—one fat and red, one tall and blue—sat on its middle. Behind them leaned the sort of frame you put on a desk, holding a picture of Mom wearing a different hairdo and laughing. The candles' shivering flames made the picture's long black hair wave like the wind was blowing it and the eyes move around as if they were looking for someone to share a joke.

"You the one give her this, if I ain't mistaken?" On Grampa Carl's unfolded palm, the pointy white feather Tupelo had chosen shone sleek and perfect.

"Yes." Winna reached for it but stopped mid-grab.

"Take it! I want you to place a wish on it and lay it on the altar—that's the towel, bootnose."

Winna took the feather. "Then will Mom be cured?"

"Didn't I say I was lookin into liftin the Burden since before she was born?" Grampa Carl shook his head no. "Too heavy for one person on his own. But I got a way to fix things so they won't get no worse.

"You be thinkin how to ask for what you want. I need to put the finishin touches on this here." He snapped his fingers. "And ain't I got just the thing—I'll be back directly."

Winna knelt down by the altar. She put her hands together with the feather between them. She would wish the best wish ever. Even if what she was going to do before wasn't technically stealing, it had been bothering her. This would help and not be wrong. A memory of Mom when she was well, dressed up and dancing with Uncle Marv at a barbecue, mixed with dreams of coming home and Mom taking her and Tupelo to the movies or out for ice cream. How should she ask for them to become real?

SLAM! Winna's muscles jerked tight. A window had banged shut in back of her. "Here we go!" Grampa Carl came out of the attic's other end, carrying a square clay pot with one of his rosemary plants growing over its sides. "This'll stand for the Earth, see?" He knelt down beside her and set the pot on the towel, behind Mom's photo. That made sense. The pot was earth and it had earth inside. "The candles is the fire and the water is the water. And the feather will be the air. All the elements." Grampa Carl nodded and leaned back. "Now. You figured out your wish?"

"Not yet."

"Don't take all day, bootnose. We ain't got it." He pulled his shaggy eyebrows down. "Ordinarily I'd a waited to light the candles till last, but Rachel was improved quite a bit when I left the hospital. Wanted to stabilize the patient and they was right to hand, so I did em soon as I come in."

He patted a place on the towel in front of the water glass. "We don't need nothin fancy, Winna. Winona didn't neither. All she did was swear her same vows twice. You can be just as simple. Whisper what you want with your breath hittin the feather. Then you gotta do it again and then you lay it on down."

"Two times? Is that so the Twins will help?"

"You catchin on, bootnose. Now get to work."

"I want my mom to stay alive," Winna muttered over the weightless whiteness. "I want my mom, Rachel Hawkes Williams, to get well and live." But instead of where Grampa Carl had said to put it, she reached past the picture frame and stuck the swan feather in the dirt of the rosemary pot. Then she wondered why.

"Well!" Grampa Carl seemed surprised. Not mad, though. "That's a good idea—rootin the wish. Air and Earth together. You are *most definitely* gettin the hang of this." For a minute they watched the candles burn and the water sparkle, the scent of the rosemary dry and sharp like a Christmas tree in the warm air.

Then Grampa Carl stood up. "Come on. I know you originally come here hopin to find out how fast them specs is repairin themselves."

Not exactly, but Winna followed him across the carpet and between the chairs to the shelves of his altar. The window there let in plain-colored late morning light—there must still be plenty of time before noon, judging by the crabapple's stretched-long circle of shadow on the grass outside. On the altar's bottom shelf was a small wood box. Grampa Carl picked it up and went to sit in the rocker. He opened it on his lap.

Inside lay a red and blue bundle, wider than the specs on their own would be. The ends of the bundle were tied with white ribbons. Grampa Carl lifted out the bundle—it looked like the wrapping cloth was a pair of sewn-together bandanas. He squeezed it like a little pillow and the same smell as the rosemary came to Winna's nose, plus others: sweetness, too, per-fumey and old and wild all at once. And some kind of fruit, tangy with wakefulness. And so much more she couldn't begin to name.

Winna touched the bundle. Her hand started humming! She pulled away and the humming kept on! She shook her hand but it wasn't asleep and the feeling didn't stop—"Grampa Carl!"

He was laughing! Only small chuckles, though, and he took her hand and held it in his two and the humming quit. "Guess that's our answer. Ain't ready, bootnose. The hoodoo still workin. Sometimes the spirits get ahead a things—they not so dependent on time like we is. Kinda like they can ignore it—but evidently that ain't the case this instance." He bent over and wiped invisible stuff from his hands onto the rug.

Winna couldn't wear the spectacles now. Her head—maybe her whole body—would buzz too hard to bear. "So when?" she asked. "Am I going to have a chance to lift the Burden before your birth—"

"Hold on a sec—hear that?" Far downstairs the phone rang. "Could be Dot callin about your mama!" Faster than she would have thought he could move, Grampa Carl disappeared through the piles of storage. By the time Winna reached the steps he had already gone on to the living room.

"Hello? Hello? Oh. Oh, I thought maybe you was news from the hospital. Yeah, Winna's here. Don't you fret. Yeah. I'll swing by and drop her off on my way to Kalamazoo, no trouble. Now hold on! Nothin happened to her, an Benny ain't to blame for ridin on ahead when she stayed behind. Ain't no need to work yourself up that way about it, Picquetta! Enough real things to worry about."

Winna worried about real things the whole ride back to Paw Paw.

# Chapter Nineteen

Next day Mom was a little better, and by Friday the doctors took her out of Intensive Care. She was still too sick for them to visit, but Gramma came home and Winna and Tupelo stopped spending the nights at Aunt Pic's.

Finally came the day when Winna was going to be able to do something: the day of the family reunion picnic. She woke up Saturday morning at Grampa Carl's and Gramma's before there was any real light in the sewing room's one window. The air looked like dark milk. But she could tell that the hall door was open. It had been shut last night. She slid out from under the hide-a-bed's covers and there beneath the turned-off lamp were the spectacles, shining, waiting. Magic again? She reached out her hand and touched them. No humming. She put them on.

No Estelle. But after all, Winna hadn't wondered whether she could see her. Yet.

In order to ask "What if" out loud and not wake up Tupelo, she had to get dressed and go somewhere else. She put on her shorts and tennis shoes and one of Aunt Pic's shrunken madras shirts over her tee shirt. Her regular glasses were in their case; she tucked them in the shirt's breast pocket and buttoned it.

She went out to the hall. The window at its other end was pink with the start of sunrise. And Grampa Carl stood in front of it as a sideways shadow. He had a finger up to his lips like he was saying "Shhh!" Then Winna heard the quiet click of the closing bedroom door. Grampa Carl came toward her and she went toward him and they met in the hallway's middle. He took her hand in the pink greyness and steered her through the kitchen and out to the pantry's back steps.

Winna looked around. With the specs on, everything was made of stories: a story about the seed in the fruit that the tree had grown from, one about the drops of water gathered into clouds of glowing red and orange and apricot and tangerine—

"Them spectacles workin all right for you now?"

"I guess they are. I haven't had time to test them, but they seem fine so far."

"Maybe you oughta wait a while. Don't want to use up all their juice. The way I had to fix em, they may not have more'n two spells left to do for you."

Only two more speculations? What if she wondered the wrong things— No, she didn't say that out loud, and she thought it only once. "You mean I won't be able to see Estelle anymore?"

"Is seein ghosts GONNA help you lift the Burden and save me and Dot's child? That's what you need to get clear on."

Maybe she was just being selfish. No. "I have to ask some questions. Get to the bottom of things."

She thought she knew where to go for that. Grampa Carl agreed. But riding her bike up the spiraling road to Covey Hill was more like getting to the top of things. When she reached the stone pillars guarding the grave-yard gates, she knocked on them again. This time no one told her to stay out. She walked between the pillars and parked her bike in the grass.

Silver coated every blade. Tiny beads of water reflected the morning's brightness. Trees by the wall held shade in their high branches, ready to drop it gently when the time for coolness came. A tiny bird flew silently out of a silver bush. Another one followed behind it as they swooped over the leaning headstones.

Now to say the formula she had created on her way here. Big breath in, then, out loud: "What if these spectacles worked the same as they did before? What if these spectacles worked the way they used to, before Cousin Benny messed them up?"

Down the road came a group of people in clothes blown by a wind that wasn't there. The tallest woman was Great-Great-Grandmother Winona, looking exactly the same. And Estelle—Estelle ran ahead of the others, a big grin on her wavery ghost face. She stopped in front of Winna and said something.

The final test. Winna huffed softly on the spectacles and—yes! Words appeared on their clouded-up lenses:

*I knew you would find a way,*    *even only for a day.*

Would the magic end tomorrow? But what did that matter? As long as she figured out how to lift the Burden first. Without putting the specs back on, Winna asked, "Why are you still here? Why isn't my mom better? I found Key. Shouldn't the Burden be lifted?"

| | |
|---|---|
| *You only did the first part* | *of what Winona swore.* |
| *She has to hold him in her arms;* | *you have to do a little more.* |

What!? Winna wanted to throw the specs in the dirt and smash them with her feet. "Are you kidding me? I found her precious hundred-year-old baby—all the way in Oregon! And still she has to kill my—kill my mom? That's not fair!"

Too mad to cry, Winna put the spectacles on her face. She looked Estelle straight in her unmoving eyes. "You tell your grandmother—no! I'll tell her myself!"

Winna marched right through Estelle to the grown-up ghosts standing together higher along the road. Great-Great-Grandmother Winona came to their front. She looked sad. Sorry. She put her hands together, folding her fingers like for a prayer. Her mouth moved; Winna thought she was saying, "Thank you."

It could be disrespectful to say to your great-great-grandmother what Winna was thinking. But Mom was dying, so she said it anyway: "If you're so grateful to me, why don't you take off your curse? I did what you said to—"

Great-Great-Grandmother Winona shook her head. She talked more, saying too much to understand by looking at her. Winna grabbed the specs off again and breathed on them but they stayed foggy, without words. Because Winna had never wondered what if she could see what any ghosts besides Estelle were saying.

Talking to Great-Great-Grandmother Winona was not going to help.

And there was probably only one more speculation left to make. And the sky was blue and white and the sun had come up completely and if Winna stayed here much longer, the excuse Grampa Carl had come up with wouldn't work and she'd get in trouble.

"I have to go back," Winna said. The ghosts followed her to the cemetery's entrance. Only Winna's feet marked the silver grass. Only her shoes touched the ground and scuffed the gravel of the cemetery's sad road.

Maybe Mom would become a ghost, too. Maybe Winna's final wish should be seeing her after she died.

At the pillars she stopped to say goodbye. Estelle pointed at the specs, so Winna took them off and huffed softly on the lenses.

*We'll come with you.*          *We can try*

> helping if               *don't cry.*
> *you want;*

Winna wasn't crying. Not a lot. Only a few tears leaked down the sides of her nose, tickling. She wiped them away angrily. "If you can come with me out of the graveyard, why can't you all go to Oregon and see Key and lift the Burden? What's the big difference?"

> *We cannot cross         where rivers run.*
>
> *But we'll be near           if you can find*
>
> *a way to make the       Burden light*
>
> *and ease                  guilty mind.*
> *Winona's*

Great-Great-Grandmother Winona felt bad? Well, she should. Mom being this sick—her own grand-daughter Estelle dying! Everything was all her fault.

Great-Great-Grandmother Winona certainly didn't look evil, though. She looked sorrowful and—and trapped! And maybe she *was* trapped? Ghosts couldn't cross rivers? Why? They could float—but Winna had only ever seen them go a short ways in the air. She had never seen one fly.

Estelle started talking again. Winna breathed on the lenses to re-fog them.

Don't blame
  Winona for the
  curse;

in some ways for
  her it's worse.

She has to hold
  Key to her heart

so he can mend
  its broken part.

It's what
  she vowed

and said out loud;

now that is what
  will have to be,

and even
  she cannot
  break free.

Which didn't seem fair. Anyone who put on a curse ought to be able to take it off whenever they felt like it.

Only this wasn't a curse. It was the Burden, a heavy load that all the Coles carried. And Winna was going to get it lifted—some way or another.

She had all the rest of the day to figure out how. She was not giving up.

"Okay. Even if I can't hear your grandmother, you can, and you can tell me what she says about my ideas, right?"

Estelle nodded hard. She grabbed her grandmother's hand and tugged her out of the group of other grown-up ghosts—who immediately looked much less interesting and much more alike.

Winna walked her bike down Covey Hill. She could probably have given both ghosts a ride since they didn't weigh anything. One on the handlebars and one on her seat—but would she see well enough then?

She and Grampa Carl had decided to tell Gramma that she was going to gather flowers as her excuse for getting out of the house. So she took the path that went off the road after two loops again, and this time she found the way to the garden behind the wall. It was as beautiful as she had imagined it: full of white honeysuckle hedges and purple milkweed and orange tiger lilies and red hollyhock, and more of the vines of pink roses. Grandpa Carl had said that the house used to be the home of that bully Ken's grandfather. Since it was abandoned, anyone could be there and they were only technically trespassing. She gathered a big bunch of flowers of every kind and laid them in her bike's basket. One of Estelle's hair ribbons would be perfect to tie the bouquet, except they weren't really there.

When she got back with them, Winna didn't know if Gramma believed the excuse or if she was too busy getting ready for the picnic to care. Last night they had made lemon cupcakes, but almost everything else had to be done today.

While Gramma was rolling out top and bottom pie crusts, Cousin Benny came over. Aunt Pic wanted him out of the way while she concentrated on Grampa Carl's birthday cake. He helped himself to Shredded Wheat and milk and sugar. Winna had it for her breakfast, too. Gramma let them add a couple of spoonfuls of cut-up strawberries from some waiting to be stirred into a filling. From the wall between the kitchen and the bathroom, Winna heard splashing sounds. Grampa Carl must be in the tub. Tupelo wandered in, still wearing her pajamas; Winna poured another bowl of cereal for her baby sister.

Great-Great-Grandmother Winona and Estelle stood out of the way by the freezer. The flowers fit in a green glass vase.

Gramma put the pies in the already hot oven and sat down at the table. "Goin to be a glorious day."

Winna would think of a way to make that true.

The bathroom door creaked open and Grampa Carl padded by in his robe. A sweet smell followed after him in the air. Winna left Tupelo slurping up soggy cereal and knocked on the bedroom door. "Enter, bootnose."

How had he known who was knocking?

Grampa Carl stood in front of the dresser combing his mustache. On the made-up bed lay the suit he was going to wear: crinkly cloth pants with thin white-and-golden-peaches stripes, and a shirt the color of vanilla ice cream. He looked at her in the mirror. "You find out what you needed?"

Winna nodded, but only a little. "Great-Aunt Estelle reminded me I have to do more to lift the Burden," she told Grampa Carl. "Because Great-Great-Grandmother Winona wants to hold her baby again." She shut her eyes tight. She was still not going to cry. "Only he's an old man now and he can't even come here and even if he did, how could she hold him since she's only a ghost!" And more hot tears leaked out between her squeezed-tight lids. But when Winna opened her eyes, she realized Grampa Carl wasn't looking at her at all—he was staring right where Estelle and her grandmother sat on the bed's white spread. He *had* to know the ghosts were there.

He set his comb on a tray of things on the dresser

top. "Believe in yourself, bootnose. You're almighty smart. And remember the Twins an their Rule of Two—you still got another speculation left, dontcha?"

"Winna!" Gramma's voice came down the hall from the bathroom. Winna had to go see what she wanted.

"There you are. Hop in the tub with your sister now. I just got time to get you two dressed and your hair done while I start the chicken to fryin."

Homemade fried chicken. If only Mom could come to the picnic to eat it. Winna set the specs on the back of the sink. Condensation was everywhere, but no use trying to run ideas by Estelle with Tupelo around. Winna sank down in the tub and helped her little sister scrub her back and rinse off. Gramma took Tupelo out and sat her on the clothes hamper to brush her hair. She made Tupelo stand on the hamper like she was a statue and stretched the neck of her sundress wide to slide over her head.

"Now go get your sandals on." Gramma opened the bathroom door, hurried Tupelo through, and shut it. Then she was back by the tub. "You ain't done yet? Find your towel and dry off and get in that dress hung on the door hook. Then come to the kitchen for your hair." She whisked out through the door and snapped it shut again.

As soon as Gramma left, Winna pulled the plug

and got out of the tub to get the specs. Time for only one question for Winona. "Maybe if you see all the people besides Key that belong to our family, that will be enough to lift the Burden?"

"Winna! How many times I have to call you!" She scrambled into her matching sundress and left the steamy bathroom.

No brush for Winna—she got the comb instead. She sat between Gramma's knees on the linoleum. She used to be jealous of Tupelo's good hair, which was in ponytails. While Gramma worked on Winna, Tupelo was allowed to frost the cupcakes.

How could Winna save Mom? The comb jerked at Winna's thick tangles in one parted-off section after another while Tupelo licked her fingers and sang choir songs. Winna really didn't mind. If only nothing sad would ever happen to make her singing stop.

Gramma finished braiding Winna's front and went to the stove to turn the chicken pieces hissing and sputtering in the frying pan's hot grease. When both sides of Winna's head were done, Gramma got up again. Winna put the specs back on. Great-Great-Grandmother Winona was hovering over the stove—still out of the way, but obviously fascinated by it. Estelle perched on the edge of the big porcelain sink, watching Gramma set cooked legs and thighs to drain on torn-open grocery bags. She might as well have sat directly *on* the chicken. She wouldn't hurt it. She was a ghost, made out of air.

At last Winna's hair was done. Gramma rubbed her knees and elbows with the Vaseline and let her get up. "But stay inside," Gramma warned her. "We're almost ready to go, and you need to keep clean, at least till we get to the park."

Where could she and the ghosts be inside alone?

The pantry was empty. Then Benny barged in. He wore a knitted shirt that looked way too sweaty, even with short sleeves. "Got any peanut butter? I'm spozed to make something to bring."

"Peanut butter?" Not picnic food—were sandwiches all he could make?

"Yeah. And celery. And raisins."

Winna stared at him.

"You never heard a Ants-on-a-Log?" It was a recipe from a Paw Paw library book, Winna remembered. She showed him where to find his ingredients and signaled for Estelle and Great-Great-Grandmother Winona to follow her to the bathroom. But Gramma was in there already. And Tupelo was curled up on the sewing room's folding bed. And the living room was on everyone's way out of the house, and the bedroom door was shut, which was the way to the attic, and when she knocked no one answered.

But the dining room was dark and empty, curtains closed. Winna pulled out chairs on three sides of the table and they all sat down.

"Okay," she said. "Will that work? That idea I came up with in the bathtub? Of having so many relatives around they're enough to lift the Burden by themselves?" She breathed and waited for her answer.

But even before the words appeared she knew. No.

*It has to be the baby Key.*          *That's what she said. It has to be.*

Both ghosts looked sorry. Both of them looked at Winna like she could save their whole world.

Maybe she could.  At the park it would be easier to slip away with them and come up with a good plan for how to use her last chance to fix everything so it came out right.

The bedroom door opened. Grampa Carl came out carrying a fancy straw hat. Smiling. If he was worried about his daughter dying, he was hiding it. "You ready, bootnose? Time to load the truck."

# Chapter Twenty

Swans floated close to the pond's edge, skimming around the green lily pads like fluffy bouquets. Nobody was frightening them to the water's middle. The same as on Memorial Day, Grampa Carl and Gramma were the first ones to get to the park. Winna thought it would be easy to find a place to go off alone and talk to the ghosts. But by the time Grampa Carl set up Gramma's chair (the only work he was allowed do on his birthday), Aunt Pic came. She went over to the ballfield with Cousin Benny, and he fired pitches at her; some she caught, and some she let bang and rattle against the backstop.

As soon as they started that, more cars drove up. Winna, and even Tupelo, had to help their Cole and

Hawkes relatives carry food to under the shady roof of the storm shelter: a big bowl of potato salad resting in a bigger bowl of ice chips, with its plastic wrap shimmering in the soft breeze; and Gramma's fried chicken; and a foil pan full of macaroni-and-cheese; and corn muffins on a plate; and a warm, heavy, slippery crockery dish holding greens with turkey necks; and hot dogs chopped up in baked beans; and orange Jell-O laced with pale flecks of miniature marshmallows, glowing like a bonfire in its clear mold; and oatmeal cookies; and sugar cookies; and molasses cookies; and the girls' own lemon cupcakes; and a roaster filled with ham; and green beans; and wax beans; and coleslaw; and sliced tomatoes sprinkled with salt and sugar; and French bread with garlic butter; and carrot sticks in vases of water; and corn on the cob wrapped in aluminum and ready to grill; and of course Cousin Benny's Ants-on-a-Log.

And afterward they would have the red velvet cake made and decorated by Aunt Pic special for Grampa Carl's birthday, and chocolate ice cream from Pastor Day's freezer chest.

Winna would wrap some cake up to keep for Mom for later.

She ate as fast as she could. Which was maybe a shame, but she had a really big problem to figure out. Making sure that Tupelo was busy with her food, Winna snuck off to the dirt path that went around the pond. On the far side she climbed a tree with enough leaves to hide her. But she could still see through its branches to the storm shelter and the parking lot.

If Great-Great-Grandmother Winona couldn't lift the Burden even now that she knew where her lost baby lived, what would Winna try next? She concentrated her imagination.

One more "what-if" left. She had to follow the Rule of Two. Eyes were an important part of the magic. Could she wonder what would happen if she saw Key Gonder walking toward the storm shelter? No, because that wouldn't have to mean he was actually *there*. People could see stuff that wasn't real. Like Tupelo's bad dream. Winna twisted around on the tree limb. The only good branch to hold was over her head. Staying stretched up to reach it made her arms ache, but she tried to ignore that.

Should she say something about seeing the Burden lifted? Same problem. Seeing the way to lift it? But she already knew that. . . .

The wind dropped from a breeze to a whisper, from a whisper to silence. The tiny ripples on the pond's surface smoothed down to a mirror, flat and reflecting the sky's blue in its blackness, the clouds above shimmering there below, too, white and strange. Two cloud reflections were moving away from the rest—moving in Winna's direction. Coming clearer. They turned from soft shapelessness into recognizable ghosts. Great-Great-Grandmother Winona and Estelle.

They floated up from the water, rising through the tree to where Winna sat. The air was so quiet. Not one leaf rustled, even when the ghosts brushed against them. Winna saw again how Estelle's face kept changing. Like smoke. All the ways she looked were worried. Estelle's grandmother, too. They pretended to sit on branches that would have been too thin if they were alive, almost twigs. The branches didn't bend.

Great-Great-Grandmother Winona said something to Estelle, who nodded. Winna let loose with one hand to fog up the specs.

*Please be glad,* *and not the other*
*Winona says,* *way around.*

*You have done a* *at least her Key is*
*lot to help;* *found.*

"So what?" Winna asked the air. "So I'm supposed to be satisfied with that? I didn't lift the Burden yet. And you—you want me to give up now? To quit and let Mom die like everyone else? Well I won't!" Her voice was loud, almost yelling. Rude. "I'm sorry." She breathed on the specs again to give Estelle a chance to say something back.

No one wants
  your ma to die;

the Burden must
  be lifted high.

We all thought
  that you

would find out
  what to do;

would come up
  with a way
  that's new

to use the Rule
  of Two.

The Rule of Two was part of the hoodoo Grampa Carl had used to make the spectacles magic. It came from those spirits Grampa Carl had called "the Twins." A new way to use their power? How should she know that? She wasn't even a plain old normal human twin, let alone a spirit one.

Marcus was. And his brother, Tony. And his mother, and his mother's sister, Miss Tooma. She would simply have to bring herself to explain to them what she needed—a new way to use the powers of these spirits— and see if they could come up with one. When, though?

Mom was out of Intensive Care, and still alive, but for how much longer?

This had to happen right away. Right now.

Only there was so much she didn't understand. Too much. Grampa Carl was old enough that he understood a lot more and even he hadn't lifted the Burden after a whole life trying.

The branches Great-Great-Grandmother Winona and Estelle sat on dipped and came up like fishing poles. Were they older than Grampa Carl? Did ghosts get old?

Maybe *they* knew the best speculation she should make. Or maybe Winna ought to speculate what would happen if they *did* know.

Maybe . . . Or if not the ghosts, then maybe the spirits? Yes. "What if the—the Twins could see and follow the best way to make my problems work out right and do it all by the end of today?" Once. "What if the Twins could do what they see and solve how to make the Coles Burden-free?" Twice. And rhyming, like Estelle's words on the spectacles. Winna hoped that would make what she said more powerful.

A shimmer went through the world almost exactly the way it had a month ago in Grampa Carl and Gramma's driveway. Only this time the rainbow colors came together instead of spreading out and apart.

Swirling tighter and tighter, disappearing to the corner of her vision.

And then the world was ordinary again. Normal. Except for the ghosts still sitting in the branches up over Winna's head.

But even they had changed: their arms were out, pointing at the parking lot. Why?

A second passed before anything else happened. Then a shiny car pulled up. Miss Ross's Mercury. The nearest door opened and she got out. Why was she riding instead of driving in her own car?

Another white lady, a stranger in a yellow dress, got out of the car's back door on the same side. The driver's door opened and a white man got out wearing a white suit with dark stripes. He opened the car's other back door, the one on the far side so Winna couldn't really see—

Estelle and Great-Great-Grandmother were gone, gliding over the grass, skipping across the pond like stones that didn't weigh anything. A man in a wheelchair came around the car's front. He wore a light brown shirt and dark brown pants. And gold glasses. As soon as she saw him, Winna was sure.

This was Key. The man in the wheelchair was her great-great-uncle, Key Gonder. The missing Key.

So the man in the suit must be Truman Gonder, who wrote that letter saying Key couldn't come. And the white—no, not white—the Negro lady who only *looked* white had to be his sister, and her name was Eleanora Gonder Forsythe. And by some miracle, they had shown up here today.

Quick as birds, the ghosts had reached the pond's far side. Winna could still see them both—then only one, Estelle, as Great-Great-Grandmother Winona held her arms out to Key and touched him and *dissolved* right into him like sugar in tea.

Winna scrambled down to the foot of the tree, but then she couldn't see anything. No fair for Estelle to have floated. She ran along the path to where the woods ended, and met her coming back. The ghost's body wavered like before, and her face, and everything but her eyes. Winna could see by those that the ghost was happy.

Winna was happy, too. The Burden of the Coles had finally been lifted! Great-Great-Grandmother Winona had held Great-Great-Uncle Key in her arms, whether he felt her or not. His mother had held him, and now her mother, Winna's mother, would be all better soon.

Maybe she still had another what-if left to use with Estelle. "Can you come play baseball with me?" She took the specs off and clouded them with her breath.

*Sorry, no.*          *I have to go.*

Go where? Wherever dead people went when they were done being ghosts, she guessed. Heaven? Winna hoped so. There was no sorrow in Heaven. It was a good place; Winna shouldn't keep Estelle from getting there.

More words appeared:

*I only came to thank you*          *for your help and say goodbye.*

*The Burden's lifted from us all.*          *Now I can leave and truly fly.*

Winna put the spectacles on again. Estelle stepped backward, into the light. The ghost's unwavering eyes looked straight into Winna's and the rest of her ghost-self became just as still. Then her mouth curved up and her arms spread like wings and she rose in the air like before, but higher and higher, rising and circling like a swan and melting into the sun. Winna followed below, watching Estelle disappear.

She wiped her face where the tears ran down and started walking again.

In a few minutes the path ended. The white—no, not white—the man who had driven the car was pushing the wheelchair slowly over weeds and grass. Miss Ross and the other lady from the car followed him. The sister had straight red hair. She marched forward like she was trying to be brave.

Winna was near enough now not to have to shout. "Hello," she said, and smiled at the lady to make her feel better. She kept walking toward them, past the shelter. That made some people look up, relations and old folks, because why was she talking to these white people nobody knew?

"Miss Winna Williams?" The man sounded like a prize announcer. "Truman Gonder, but you may call me Uncle True. I assume you received at least one of our telegrams? Highly pleased to make your acquaintance." So why did he look mad, then? He stopped his chair-pushing and shook hands with her like she was a grown-up. He must be angry at someone else. Maybe at whoever had been supposed to deliver the telegrams.

Miss Ross wore a pink hat like a wreath of roses. "Winna, this is Mrs. Forsythe."

"Eleanora," said the lady who wasn't white.

Well, Winna wasn't going to call her by just her first name. "You're my aunt?"

The lady's face turned bright red. "Yes, I guess I am." She jabbed her hand out and held it for Winna to shake like her brother had. "We hope you don't mind that we took you up on your invitation after all. We received a windfall—an inheritance earlier contested by my deceased husband's brother. But also there was a . . . development. A rather . . . disgusting phone call—"

"The whole business was a pack of nonsense." Uncle True made a face like he wanted to spit. "Claiming Grandfather Key wasn't—was—"

"Why do you insist on talking *about* me? Talk *to* me! I keep telling you I'm right here!" Great-Great-Uncle Key circled his wheelchair around so he sat facing his grandchildren. "Rumors of my death are greatly exaggerated!" He winked at Winna. "You understand what that means, don't you?"

"Exaggerating is lying so something seems bigger," she said. Exaggerate was one of the longest words she knew.

Great-Great-Uncle Key nodded. "That's right. Smart little girl, aren't you? Stands to reason."

"Winna!" She twisted around and saw Grampa Carl and Tupelo coming to meet these new people. Tupelo suddenly let loose of Grampa Carl's hand and ran ahead. She stopped in front of Great-Great-Uncle Key and stared at him for a whole minute, totally ignoring Miss Ross introducing her.

"What's wrong with you?" asked Tupelo, pointing at the wheelchair.

"Nothing that a time machine couldn't fix," Great-Great-Uncle Key answered. "What's wrong with you?"

"Nuffing!" Tupelo stuck her chin out. "Nuffing's wrong!"

"Oh, I don't know! Seems to me there's something . . . stuck . . . right"—he reached beneath Tupelo's left side ponytail with one shaking freckled hand—". . . right here!"—and pulled out a strawberry Tootsie Pop! Tupelo took it from him.

"I didn't hear any thank-yous," said Grampa Carl's voice over her shoulder. Winna realized her mouth was as wide open as Tupelo's and they had both forgotten their manners.

"Never mind all that," said Great-Great-Uncle Key. "I take it you're another of my relatives?"

"Carl Ezekiel Hawkes. By marriage only. Welcome to Vandalia."

"Carl? The birthday boy?" Maybe if you were over a hundred years old, Grampa Carl could be a boy. He took his hat off and bowed to Great-Great-Uncle Key and Miss Ross and Aunt Eleanora and Uncle True, and helped push the wheelchair to the shelter where Gramma waited to fix them all plates.

The grown-ups talked. Once Great-Great-Uncle Key had read Winna's letter, he insisted that they come to the reunion, no matter what the plane tickets cost. It had something to do with how pretty soon it would be too late for him to travel anywhere, because he'd be gone. That was a little confusing, but Winna figured out what they meant: sometimes it was more polite to say gone than dead.

There was no phone number on the letter they'd gotten, so Aunt Eleanora had made Uncle True send two telegrams: one to Grampa Carl's and Gramma's house, and one to the genealogy club's crossed-out address on the envelope they got. Miss Ross got the club one, so she went to the Kalamazoo airport to meet them. Since no one else came to pick them up and they were invited in writing, she brought the Gonders here to Vandalia for the picnic.

It had all worked out.

Grampa Carl rolled Great-Great-Uncle Key's wheelchair to their main picnic table, the one where Winna had placed the picked flowers. The chair fit fine on the table's end, where there weren't any benches.

Cousin Benny came back from practicing on the ballfield and shoved himself down between Winna and Great-Great-Uncle Key. He gave Winna half of an apology and half of an explanation: "Gotta conduct my final interview." He took a paper napkin from the pile by the flowers and started writing on it with a pencil. "Number one: When you first understood who you really are?"

Great-Great-Uncle Key folded his hands on his

stomach and closed his eyes. Winna thought he was going to answer until his soft snoring started.

Cousin Benny snorted and closed his eyes, too. But then he opened them and looked across the picnic table at Uncle True. "You the victim's son?"

"What? Who's a victim?"

"Kidnap victim. Key Gonder."

"Ah! No, I—" Uncle True gazed at Cousin Benny like the boy was a biting dog.

"This is Mr. Truman Gonder. He's Great-Great-Uncle Key's *grand*son," Winna said.

"Oh. Hunh. How do? You got anything to add to the case?"

"The—"

Winna explained. She made Benny sound more important than he had been and used his story about finding diaries. After a while Uncle True acted a little more relaxed.

"What do you do when you're not cracking century-old kidnapping cases, Benjamin?"

Benny smiled like he believed everything Winna had said about him. "Trainin to be a pitcher. I'm the best. I beat any team ever comes against me, every time."

He stood up and folded the napkin so it fit in his shirt pocket. "See you on the field, Winna. Joanie Jergens is better, and I got Tony and Marcus Tate promised to come, so I guess you gonna be on the losin side this time."

She didn't say anything back as Cousin Benny left the storm shelter, though she did think to herself, "Pride goeth before a fall." That was in the Bible.

Aunt Pic opened the box she had brought Grampa Carl's cake in and Gramma was putting on its candles. So the ice cream should be here soon.

"You're quite the impressive young lady," said Uncle True, wiping his head with a napkin. The stripes on his suit were dark blue. He was bald. The skin on his scalp shone pink.

"Did you always know you were colored?" she blurted out. More bad manners. She should have said thanks for the compliment. "I mean—"

"It's all right. I understand—I've been a tad nervous myself." He wiped his napkin across his forehead. "Well. There were stories in the family. Stories about a secret. You know Grandfather was raised with a different name, don't you? Elihu Gilkie. Everyone had heard how he changed it to what it is now, Key Gonder, when he moved out West and married Grandmother, but we had no notion why, no clue that was his real name. He only told us it was because of a disagreement with Great-Grandfather Gilkie, his father—his adopted father, I guess. Great-Grandfather must have told him his real name when they fought. The story Grandfather had been given was that he was the natural son of Great-Aunt Amelia, Great-Grandmother Anne Gilkie's long-lost sister, and he got treated like second-best due to being born out of wedlock.

"Now we know the truth. Of course. But even when your letter came, the idea that we were—were colored didn't occur to me *or* my sister. Remember, you didn't say one syllable on the subject. And it wasn't till we saw Miss Ross's report—very touching, and Grandfather assures us it's accurate based on what he's been able to gather—but we never saw that report till after we received a telephone call from our Tate cousins, warning us not to pay it any attention. Then . . . That's when Grandfather insisted on us attending the birthday party and taking him along, if it was the last trip he made."

Winna did her best to understand what Uncle True was saying. He had gotten a call from Marcus and Tony Tate claiming Winona's Tale was a lie. That was when Truman and Eleanora finally told Great-Great-Uncle Key about the letter, and he told them the story must be right. So then Great-Great-Uncle Key made them bring him to visit Vandalia after they said they wouldn't. The spirit Twins got the Tate twins to lift the Burden without realizing it. Days before she even asked.

That must be how spirits worked sometimes. Like Grampa Carl had said.

If it had worked. Of course it had. Hopefully they could leave to call the hospital and check on Mom once they ate their cake and ice cream—why was it taking so long to bring it over from the pastor's freezer? She looked across the street and saw Aunt Pic and Mrs. Day on the pastor's front steps, waving their arms and jumping up and down, and she heard them shouting, too, but shouting what? Aunt Pic had the phone up over her head, holding the bottom and the receiver, and now Winna could tell she was calling for Daddy, that was Grampa Carl, to come talk long distance, and Winna knew. She *knew*. That was her mom on the phone. Grampa Carl was walking through the park already; he had a head start, but Winna ran as fast as her long legs could carry her and she beat him. And yes, it was Mom.

And yes, she was getting well, and so fast, and none of the doctors understood why. But Winna did.

"They're letting me leave tomorrow." Still her voice sounded like you'd be able to see through it, but not like something rotting apart. Now it was more like the wings of a new moth.

"Are we—you can go home? We can be home again?" Home. Together. Before she could hear her mom say yes, Grampa Carl came and Winna had to hand the phone to him. Without any shame whatsoever, Winna stayed right there, listening in to overhear his every word. At first he only went "Mmm-hmm," and "Yep." Then, "Well, that'd be a real treat! I'll tell Dot and the girls—no, it's going to be fine! No! I'll let her know as soon as I hang up." He said goodbye without asking Winna if she wanted to get back on.

That was okay, though, because of what he told her. Winna got to find it out first.

Mom couldn't go home to Kalamazoo yet. She wasn't *that* well. But tomorrow Grampa Carl and Gramma were picking her up at the hospital and bringing her to stay here. In Vandalia. For a long, long visit—all summer.

And Winna and Tupelo would get to stay there with her. Not go to California.

Winna helped carry the ice cream tub back across the street to the storm shelter. She waited politely while Grampa Carl blew out every candle on his cake. She knew he had gotten his wish. She ate her piece slowly, and the ice cream, too, letting it melt to the thickness of frosting. No hurry now to get back to Grampa Carl's and Gramma's house and use the phone. No need to call the hospital. Her mom was much, much better, and Winna would see her soon. Tomorrow.

Because she hadn't given up.

Meanwhile, she had at least a whole afternoon and evening of the spectacles' restored magic to enjoy. And apparently that still included playing the most perfect baseball in the recorded history of the world. Joanie Jergens and Marcus and Tony Tate showed up without making a single bit of difference. Winna hit two line-drive triples and a home run before Benny decided to give her automatic walks. Her team beat his 11 to 2.

# Author's Note on Where This Book Happens

Kalamazoo, Michigan, is where I was born, in 1955, a long, long time ago. Before that, my father's family lived in Vandalia and the nearby town of Cassopolis. My mother's family lived close to Paw Paw, in a little village of only 150 people, and my grandmother and grandfather are buried in Covey Hill Cemetery.

But in real life, none of these places are exactly the way I describe them in *Speculation*. If you look them up, you'll see that they're not even in the same spots on the map where I put them in what I've written.

Here's what I want this book to do: I want it to make you feel like you're in this imaginary world that I've created based on how the friends and relatives I grew up with thought and talked and acted, on where they slept and worked and fought and played. If it's doing that, good. Don't worry about matching its locations up mile-for-mile with real ones with the same names. Just be glad that you've redeemed my dear old dreams and found a beautiful new home for your own.

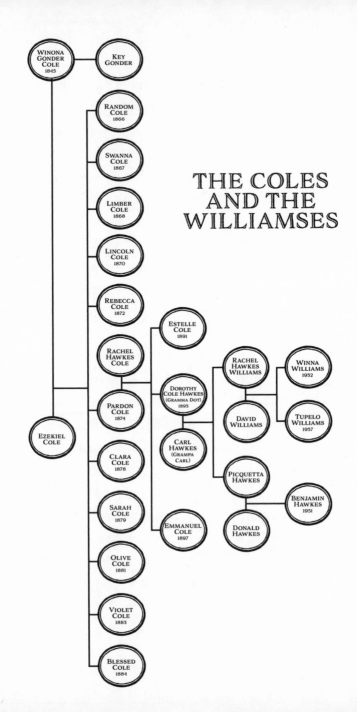

THE COLES
AND THE
WILLIAMSES

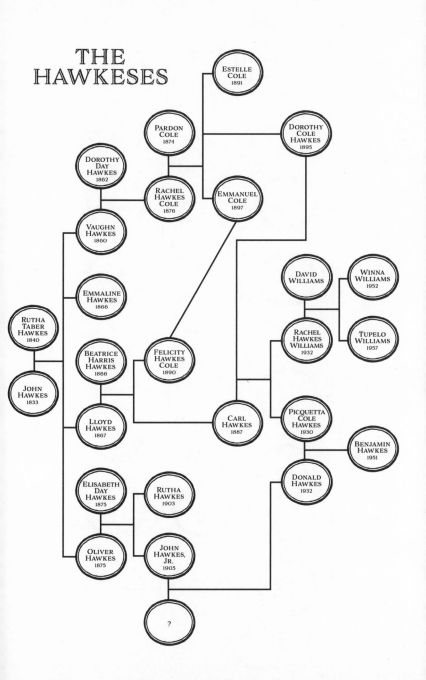

# THE GILKIES, TATES, AND GONDERS

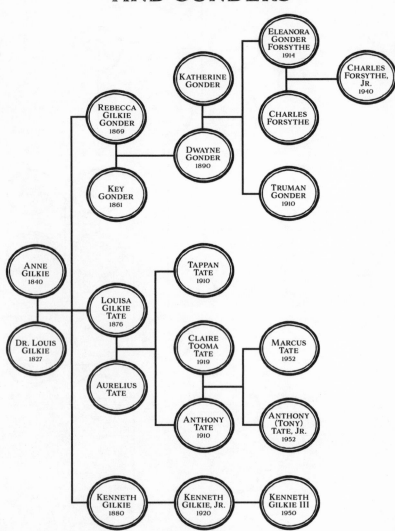